THE OWLS
HAVE COME
TO TAKE
US AWAY

THE
OWLS
HAVE COME
TO TAKE
US AWAY

RONALD L. SMITH

Clarion Books
Houghton Mifflin Harcourt
Boston   New York

Clarion Books
3 Park Avenue
New York, New York 10016

Clarion Books is an imprint of Houghton Mifflin Harcourt Publishing Company.

hmhco.com

The text was set in Minion Pro.

Library of Congress Cataloging-in-Publication Data
Names: Smith, Ronald L. (Ronald Lenard), 1959– author.
Title: The owls have come to take us away / Ronald L. Smith.
Description: Boston ; New York : Clarion Books, Houghton Mifflin Harcourt, [2019] |
Summary: After something strange happens during a camping trip,
twelve-year-old alien-obsessed Simon suspects he has been abducted,
but was it real or just his overactive imagination?
Identifiers: LCCN 2018051971 (print) | LCCN 2018056564 (ebook) |
ISBN 9781328526892 (E-book) | ISBN 9781328841605 (hardback)
Subjects: | CYAC: Alien abduction—Fiction. | Extraterrestrial beings—Fiction. |
Family life—Fiction. | Children of military personnel—Fiction. |
Military bases—Fiction. | Racially-mixed people—Fiction. | Science fiction. |
BISAC: JUVENILE FICTION / Horror & Ghost Stories. |
JUVENILE FICTION / Social Issues / Bullying. | JUVENILE FICTION /
Science Fiction. | JUVENILE FICTION / Action & Adventure / General. |
JUVENILE FICTION / Family / General (see also headings under Social Issues).
Classification: LCC PZ7.1.S655 (ebook) | LCC PZ7.1.S655 Owl 2019 (print) |
DDC [Fic]—dc23
LC record available at https://lccn.loc.gov/2018051971

Manufactured in the United States of America
DOC 10 9 8 7 6 5 4 3 2 1
4500746654

For Lynne Polvino

THE OWLS
HAVE COME
TO TAKE
US AWAY

PART ONE

CHAPTER ONE

I FIRST STARTED FREAKING OUT over aliens when I read a book of my dad's called *Communion*. The cover showed an alien with big bug eyes and a little slit for a mouth. The nose was just two tiny pinpricks. Dad said it was all make-believe — that the author was crazy, that he needed to see a doctor — but once I started reading, I couldn't stop.

The aliens I'm talking about are called Grays. They come from a binary star system called Zeta Reticuli. It's about forty light-years from Earth. They've been coming here for ages, all the way back to Egyptian times.

There are other types of aliens, too. The Reptilians — who look like lizards. The Nordics — who are tall and blond and resemble humans. But the ones that scare me the most are the Grays.

Grays.

Just saying it freaks me out.

It's such a simple word. A color. Not black or white. But something in between. Something unknowable. Something that makes me not want to sleep.

In the book, the Grays come to Earth and take this guy on one of their spaceships. They do a bunch of experiments on him and then let him go. But before they do, they put an implant under his skin so they can track him. Just like we do to animals.

Animals.

That's what we are to them.

Lab rats.

Have you ever seen those pictures of weird crop circles in cornfields? Or heard about cows being cut open and dissected? The aliens do that, too. No one knows why.

I'm going to stop now because I'm really freaking myself out.

My dad is in the Air Force, and we live in what's called base housing. All the houses look the same. Everything we need is right here: a commissary, which is what you'd call a grocery store. The BX, which stands for *base exchange* — kind of like a small department store. There's a swimming pool, a movie theater, a library, even a McDonald's. And there are rules, too. Lots of them. If you don't cut your grass, someone will come by and tell you to do it. You can only water your lawn at 1800 hours. (That's military time for six o'clock.) You can't play loud music in your backyard. And soldiers in crisp, white uniforms come by without warning and inspect the inside of your house. They want to make sure you're not living like a slob or growing marijuana in your basement. A guy in school named Jerry Finfinger had marijuana in his basement, and his dad was arrested and his family kicked off the base. What would that be like, I wondered, to have to live out there? With them. Civilians.

I knew there was a world beyond the main gates of the Air Force base, where men with guns stood at attention all day long and checked cars coming in, but I'd never been outside of it, except for family trips. It was huge out there, with crazy highways and giant stores and parking lots. Kids got kidnapped all the time. But here on the base we were safe. Safe from the outside world. And the Grays. The Air Force had weapons that could probably defeat them if they ever attacked.

One time I asked Dad if he knew anything about aliens, or if any of his pilot friends ever talked about them. He said the only alien he knew was a man named Danny Bones, who once drank thirty-three beers in one night.

I don't believe him, though. The Air Force is known for keeping secrets. All you have to do is look up Roswell.

This is what happened:

A UFO crash-landed in Roswell, New Mexico, in 1947. The

5

Air Force quickly covered it up, and said it was a hot air balloon. But that was a lie. Before they sealed off the area, several farmers found some wreckage — shiny pieces of silver, like metal or steel. There was something strange about it, though. You could ball it up in your fist like aluminum foil and then it would just uncrumple back into shape, as smooth as a sheet of paper. And there was writing on it, too. *Alien writing.* All those pieces are stored away now at Area 51, a top secret military base in the Nevada desert. And you know what else they found?

Bodies.

Alien bodies.

Grays.

One of them was still alive, but really messed up from the crash. They took him to see the president, a man named Harry Truman. The alien didn't speak, but they were able to communicate through reading each other's minds. That's called telepathy. They made a deal: The aliens would share their super-duper advanced technology if the government allowed them to take humans every now and then for their experiments. They were a dying race and needed to find ways to continue their species.

But the aliens broke their promise.

They started taking more and more people.

And there was nothing we could do about it.

CHAPTER TWO

"SIMON?" MOM CALLED up the stairs. "Are you ready?"

I groaned inside.

Earlier that day, Mom said we had to go to the BX to get some new jeans and some other stuff. "You're growing like a reed," she'd told me. She said all kinds of old-timey things like that. I didn't even know what half of them meant.

I leaned in closer to the computer screen. *Great.* Mom had fantastic timing. A hive of flying revenants was headed in my direction. I smashed my finger down on the Attack key, unleashing a fury of spells. "C'mon!" I shouted. *Zap! Fizz!* A swarm of them went down in a cloud of purple dust. I ran from the battle site and hid near a gurgling river, away from any more threats.

My character in *EverCraft* is a level-thirty High Elf Druid. His name is Rowyn. I use nature spells to defend the realm from Orzag, the Emperor of Bloodbane Forest. He was once a king, but got corrupted by a sorcerer and sold his soul. Now he's wreaking havoc on all the townspeople. (I got that from a book I read: "wreaking havoc.")

I like playing druids because they're smart, not just big brawlers. You can always tell what somebody's like in real life by what kind of character they play in a game. If you're a bully, you're definitely going to pick an ogre or a berserker, someone who's into smashing stuff. But if you're like me, what my mom calls "shy and withdrawn," you'll choose a high elf or a gnome. Someone with brains. Someone who can think things through.

I also like druids because they get a lot of cool-looking robes and spell effects. And you know what else? They can turn into wolves. That's right, *wolves*. When I'm in wolf form, I can run faster and take more damage. There's one spell I use called Thistle Protection that makes these thorny spikes bloom from my skin. You should see it. There's also a robe that gives me more mana. That's the stuff your character uses to cast spells. If you run low on mana, you can't cast any magic. Plus, there's the jewelry, rings, and magic totems. All of them give added powers.

"Simon!" Mom's voice boomed from downstairs. "Let's go. *Now!*"

I groaned and shut down the computer.

"Thought you'd never get down here," Mom said. She looked a little ticked off, but I wasn't buying it. I've never even seen her mad. "'Cool as a cucumber,'" Dad always calls her. Why are cucumbers cool? Because they're kept in the refrigerator? I don't get it.

Mom took a last sip of coffee and grabbed the car keys from the kitchen counter, and we headed out.

On the way to the BX, we passed where Dad works. It's called the Ninth Airlift Squadron. The whole area is enclosed by a giant barbed-wire fence. He loads planes with cargo and weapons that fly to military bases all over the world. Or "hot spots," he sometimes calls them. I'm sure he does other stuff too, but I don't know what that could be. He was in the Iraq War, but that was before I was born. He never talks about it. When I asked him what it was like over there, all he ever said was "War is hell, son."

I leaned my head against the car window. Row after row of identical houses flashed past. They looked like Legos. Sometimes I felt like the whole Air Force base was just one big experiment from the government, like an ant farm, and they were probably watching us right now through some kind of giant magnifying lens and taking notes.

The lights inside the BX were too bright, and the AC was too cold. People go nuts around here with the AC. Everybody's house is like a refrigerator.

Some kind of awful music was blaring from the speakers. I read somewhere that stores use certain types of music to make people relax. They think that if you're relaxed, you'll spend more money. That's pretty creepy, if you ask me.

Mom grabbed a shopping cart and started steering it down the aisle. One of the wheels was wobbly and made this *ratchety* sound that was driving me crazy.

Ratchet

Ratchet

Ratchet

We passed mountains of camping gear and a huge tower of wind-up radios with alarms and flashing lights. Everyone has to be prepared in the military for any kind of emergency. We have tons of bottled water in our basement.

I lagged behind, hoping I wouldn't see anybody from school. No one wants to get caught with their mom shopping for clothes. I slipped off to go check out the computers.

Right when I was getting kind of bored, Mom found me and dragged me back to the boys' department. She'd picked out three different pairs of jeans, and I had to try them all on. It was awful. At least she didn't go in the dressing room with me. She pulled the waist of the jeans while I had them on and made me turn around so she could see how they fit. God, it was embarrassing. *Having your mom touch your butt in public? Jeez.* I didn't really care what kind of clothes I had, as long as they were comfortable.

Mom reminded me we were going camping soon, and said I'd need some new stuff to wear. I got a couple T-shirts and a new pair of sneakers. They weren't cool sneakers, like some of the guys at school wore — Air Jordans and Converse and Vans — these were rejects. They were shaped like fish heads. I looked at the price tag. Four dollars. Jeez.

Mom plucked a baseball cap off a rack and put it on my head. "To protect you from the sun," she said.

A lot of people think that if you're black, you can't get sunburned. I'm living proof that's not true. Well, to tell the truth, I'm *half* black. Mom is black, and Dad is white. They call it biracial. I don't know who came up with that term, but I don't like it too much. If it were up to me, we'd all just be humans, and leave it at that.

I think I got more of Dad's genes, because I'm what they call light-skinned. But Mom says that's not the way it works. She says that black people come in all kinds of shades. So yeah, I've burned in the sun before. One time we were at the beach, and I got so burnt Mom kept me in the house for a week.

I followed her to the register. The wheels on the cart were

still making the *ratchety* sound, and she didn't even seem to notice. She just hummed to herself like she didn't have a care in the world.

Mom took our stuff out of the cart and started laying it out on the conveyor belt. The cashier looked about a hundred years old. A bunch of buttons in bright colors were pinned to her uniform. Actually, it was a vest. I felt bad for her. *Why would somebody make an old person wear a vest like that?*

The cashier scanned our stuff, and my eyes drifted over to a display where they kept all the magazines. A bunch of hats were hung up on a tall pole next to it. "How 'bout one of these?" I said, grabbing one that looked like something you'd wear on a safari. Mom cocked her head. "Okay. Sure, Simon. You look like an explorer."

I took off the baseball cap she'd put on my head a minute ago and set it on the pole, even though that wasn't where it was supposed to go.

I froze.

The picture on the cap showed a spaceship, with a pair of alien eyes bugging out of the window.

I let out a breath.

People think it's funny, you know? All this alien stuff. Like it's some kind of cartoon or something. But it's not funny. It's the government's way of preparing us for Full Disclosure.

That's the day when they admit the existence of UFOs and aliens.

They want us to get used to the idea first so everyone doesn't freak out when they come.

CHAPTER THREE

IN OUR LIVING ROOM, there's a framed picture of my mom standing next to a Christmas tree, holding me in her arms. I'm squirming like crazy, trying to climb my way out of her grip. There's snow outside — great big drifts of it. The tree branches through the window look like they've been dipped in white cake frosting.

I don't even know where that picture was taken. Growing up in the military, I've lived in a lot of places I don't even remember. I was born in Maine, but when I try to think of it, all I see in my head is snow. It sits on top of car hoods and trash dumpsters, mailboxes and frozen playground jungle gyms.

We've also lived in Illinois, Ohio, South Carolina, and Michigan. The only thing I remember from most of those places is being in school for a year or two and then suddenly leaving. All the names and faces of my friends just kind of blur together, like some kind of wacky kaleidoscope. Sometimes I think I shouldn't even make friends, because in a couple of years, Dad will be stationed someplace else, and we'll have to move all over again. It's all just one big bummer, if you ask me.

When I was four or five years old, I really didn't understand why we moved all the time and cried when we started packing. It got to the point where I cried every time Mom or Dad left the house, because I thought they weren't coming back.

It took me a while to get over that.

School's been out for a week, and Dad says we're going camping as soon as he gets a break at work, so it could be any day now. He loves what he calls "the great outdoors." It's all he ever talks about. He goes on and on about fishing and hunting and camping. I don't like any of those things. One time, he took me fishing, and I didn't want to put the worm on the hook, but he made me do it. I felt terrible, and still have dreams about the way the worm squirmed and wriggled.

Dad and my big brother, Edwin, went camping a couple of times, but I didn't want to go. Mom was on my side, and said that all of the pollen would probably give me an asthma attack. That only worked once, and now I have to pay for it. We were going, and there was no way out of it.

I don't really like being outside. I'd rather play video games. In the summer, it gets so hot out I feel like I can't breathe, and I have to take medicine. I use an inhaler. It's called Alupent. I don't use it a lot, but when the air gets so thick it's like walking into syrup, I have to take a few puffs. One time I got so sick they had to take me to the emergency room, where they put a mask over my face and had me breathe in this misty white stuff.

There's something else I remember, too. When I was lying in the hospital bed, with a bright light shining in my eyes and doctors standing above me, I felt trapped. I wondered if that was what it felt like to be abducted.

Helpless.

Alone.

Fortunately, that was the only asthma attack I ever had. I don't even remember what brought it on. I think it was some kind of food or dairy product or something I had at school. When it first came over me, kids started laughing while I gasped for air, but one of the teachers saw what was happening and called the nurse. Now sometimes in school, when people see me, they'll grab their throats like they're choking for air. "Gnnnuuuhh!" they'll croak out and fall to their knees. "Argghh!"

I swear, they're a bunch of a-holes.

I'm not supposed to use that word.

Dad thought I'd be into sports, like Edwin. He made me sign up for baseball, where I never got a hit, and football, where I rode the bench. We even tried soccer, which I kind of liked, but wasn't very good at. Now I hate *all* sports. I couldn't even climb the rope at gym. Everyone laughed at me — even the gym teacher, Mr. Davenport. That didn't seem right. He was an ex-Marine with a shaved head, and I swear he had muscles in his eyebrows. When he blew his whistle and forced us to run laps or do push-ups, his face turned red and a vein on his forehead throbbed like it was going to burst. He was horrible. And even though I had asthma, he never cut me a break. If anyone complained and said they couldn't do something, he'd give them a hall pass to see the nurse. Believe me, you wouldn't want to be caught with it. Know why? It was cut from a big piece of wood and shaped like a poop emoji.

Edwin's a senior now and is in Germany for some kind of soccer camp. He's one of the best players in our school district. He's good at everything. Even his teeth are perfect. Everyone wants to be his friend. He's always been pretty nice to me, even though we're nothing alike. I know he's Dad's favorite. He'd never say it out loud, but deep down inside, I know it's true. You should see them tossing the football back and forth in the backyard. Dad grins like an idiot and throws the ball so fast it'd knock me over if I tried to catch it. But Edwin catches it every time. Every. Freakin'. Time. "Way to go, champ," Dad praises him. "Good catch, buddy."

Dad and Edwin forced me to play a basketball game called HORSE one day, and I didn't make any shots. Dad only looked at me and shook his head. That made me feel bad. Sometimes, when I'm lying in bed, I think I'm just a gigantic disappointment to him.

I want to tell you something else, too.

I've never told anyone before, and only my parents know. Even though I'm twelve years old, sometimes, when I wake up in the morning, the sheets are wet. I can't help it. It ticks my dad off. He says that when I feel like I have to go, I should just get up and go to the bathroom. But it's not like that, I tell him. *I'm asleep.* Knocked out. I don't even feel it happening. All I know is I wake up and there it is: wet sheets. Mom tries to make me feel better about it. She says it's not my fault and it's just something I need to grow out of, but I don't know if that'll ever happen. That's why I never spend the night at anyone's house. *Could you imagine that?* Waking up to wet sheets at your friend's house? I don't think I'd ever recover.

Speaking of friends, I have exactly one, and his name's Tony Deaver. He's in Mexico for the summer with his parents. I tried to text him a couple of times, but the messages didn't go through. He's a pretty cool guy. He's into sports, but he's still okay. We used to play Swords and Secrets all the time. It was a game we made up based on a fantasy book we both read. Mom bought me a cloak and a fake beard. I was a wizard, like Gandalf in *The Lord of the Rings.* Dad even cut and sanded a piece of wood in his workshop so it looked like a sword. I wrapped it in aluminum foil and used my belt loop as a sheath. You should see Dad's workshop. It's in the basement. He's got about a dozen hammers. A million screwdrivers. Stacks of lumber that go all the way up to the ceiling. I swear, he could open his own Home Depot if he wanted to. He's got these little cabinets with every kind of nail, screw, nut, and bolt you can imagine. One time he showed me his collection of grommets. *What's a grommet? What's it do?* I couldn't get up the courage to ask him, though, so I just nodded along, like I knew what a damn grommet was. I had to go inside and look it up on the freakin' Internet. This is what a grommet looks like, if you ever need one:

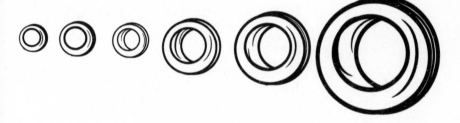

His prize possessions, though, are his power tools. I'd tell you what kind they are, but I really don't know. They just make a lot of noise.

Anyway, Tony and I used to head out to the woods behind the school and make up these crazy stories where we had to find some magic rock or crystal or whatever. It was pretty boring, actually. One day, Tony said he didn't want to play anymore.

He said it was dumb. We started playing MMORPGs instead. That stands for Massively Multiplayer Online Role-Playing Games. We played *Star Stations* and *Runes of Alamara* and *EverCraft*. I had to admit, playing video games was a lot more fun than tramping around in the woods. I didn't have to leave the house, but I could still travel to worlds a million miles away.

The one thing that's helped me to not think about aliens is writing my own fantasy stories. I haven't shown them to anyone yet, not even Tony. I'm sure Mom would be proud of me, but I'm not ready to do it. The one I'm working on now is called *Max Hollyoak and the Tree of Everwyn*. It's about this kid who's half faerie.

Okay, I know what you're thinking. *Faeries? Like Tinker Bell?* Wrong. These faeries are more like the elves in *The Lord of the Rings* — tall and noble and fierce warriors. Anyway, this kid in the book, Max Hollyoak, finds out that he has faerie blood and then goes on this big adventure.

Maybe I'll let you read some of it.

Maybe. I'll think about it.

CHAPTER FOUR

MOM MADE PANCAKES the morning after the trip to the BX. "Just the way you like them," she said. "With lots of blueberries."

The smell rose in my nostrils and made my mouth water. She placed a plate in front of me and then sat down and sipped her coffee. She does that sometimes, just sitting and staring. I guess I don't mind too much. Dad always wakes up at the crack of dawn and showers, shaves, and is out the door while I'm still sleeping.

"So, what's up for today, sweetie?" Mom asked.

"I don't know," I said. "Guess I'll play some video games or something."

She sighed and pressed her lips together. "It's a nice day, Simon. Why don't you go out and get some fresh air?"

I poured a glob of maple syrup onto my pancakes. I knew that voice. It was the one she used when she was frustrated. After a moment, she said, "I know Tony's in Mexico, but what about Billy Hampton? You haven't seen him in ages."

I froze, fork halfway to my mouth. "Mom, Billy Hampton tried to flush my head down the toilet. Remember?"

Her face fell.

It was true. Billy Hampton was a kid I used to like until he grew into a giant in what seemed like a few short weeks. He started hanging around with guys who liked to bang you up against your locker and take your lunch money. I guess he had something to prove, because one day, he found me in the bathroom and tried to give me a swirly. That's when someone sticks your head down the toilet and flushes it. It was awful, and it smelled like — well, you know what. I held my breath, hoping I wouldn't have an asthma attack. Lucky for me, I was saved at the last minute by Mr. Sofio, the science teacher. Every now and then, teachers would pop into the boys' bathrooms and catch people cutting class or doing something they weren't supposed to be doing. Like stuffing nerdy kids' heads down the toilets.

Mom made a little sound in her throat — somewhere between a gasp and a chirp. She set down her coffee cup. It read NO MAN WAS EVER SHOT WHILE DOING DISHES. "I'm sorry, honey," she said. "Maybe it's time you made some new friends."

I groaned inside. She just didn't get it. "I can't just *make* friends, Mom. There's a whole thing involved."

She didn't know that making friends at school was harder than freakin' pre-algebra. You couldn't just go up to somebody and say, "Hey, wanna be my friend?" You'd probably get punched.

I spent the rest of the day in my room playing video games and working on my Max Hollyoak book. Oh, yeah. I said I'd show you some of it, right? Okay. Well, here it is.

Remember: IT'S NOT FINISHED YET!!

Max Hollyoak and the Tree of Everwyn

I

A Frozen Pond

Max Hollyoak stepped onto the frozen pond.

His black and white dog, Alix, stamped the hard ground where she paced, now and then letting out a small whimper. Max sniffed and wiped his nose with the back of a gloved hand.

His father was dead.

Dead.

The word rang in his head like a hammer on an anvil.

He glanced at the bare trees on the other side of the pond, then looked down at his boots. Slowly, like watercolors spreading onto a canvas, an image appeared on the ice. Max blinked and shook his head.

A white flag waved in an unfelt breeze. At its very center, a proud black horse reared up on its hind legs, fire blazing from its nostrils.

The ice split apart with a terrible crack.

Max's left foot plunged into a hole. Alix barked wildly, running back and forth along the shoreline. Max threw his weight onto his right foot and yanked himself free, immediately crashing onto his butt. He scrambled backwards, wondering when the ice would shatter and he would sink into a cold, wet tomb.

Finally, he felt solid ground beneath him and climbed up the small bank and collapsed. His wet pants and shoes weighed him down. Alix whined and nudged him with her head, licking his face with a big red tongue.

"It's okay, girl," he said, breathing hard. "It's all right."

Finally, he rose, and with ice and snow crunching under his frozen sneakers, headed through the woods, back to his house.

Max shoved his hands deep into his pockets. He passed houses with warm lights burning inside and shadows moving behind the windows. He thought of the families gathered around their tables for dinner and realized his life would never be the same.

It's all my fault, he thought. *If it hadn't been for me, Dad would still be alive.*

So that's the first chapter. I have a lot more, but, like I said, I'm still working on it. I could tell you what happens next, but then that would be a spoiler, right?

CHAPTER FIVE

ONE OF THE FIRST recorded cases of UFO abduction happened a long time ago, in the 1960s. A man and woman named Betty and Barney Hill were driving home to Portsmouth, New Hampshire, when they saw a strange light in the sky. At first they thought it was a falling star and kept driving, but suddenly they saw it again. The light wasn't a star. It was a UFO, and it had stopped right in the middle of the road in front of them.

Barney looked through his binoculars and saw several small figures staring back at him through the UFO's window. That's when things got even stranger. He felt a command inside his head that told him not to move and to keep looking.

The next thing they knew, they were driving again, but they felt weird, like tired and sleepy and stuff. When they got home, they noticed that a bunch of hours had disappeared. This is called Missing Time in UFO research. After that night,

Betty started having strange dreams of being taken from the car by men who didn't seem human. Her husband said he had some sort of "mental block" and couldn't remember anything. Finally, she and her husband were hypnotized to recover their memories of that night. When she was under hypnosis, Betty remembered being on the ship, where she and Barney were put through a bunch of medical tests by the aliens. They were both terrified but couldn't do anything about it. They were frozen.

Betty remembered asking one of the aliens where they were from, and he showed her a map of stars. And you know what? Years later, an astronomer discovered a group of stars that matched her description!

That proves it really happened, right? I mean, how could she have drawn a star map that astronomers didn't even know about? Here's a picture of it:

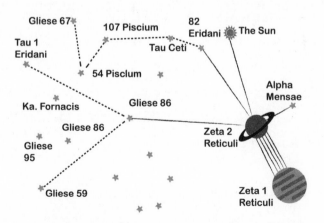

The aliens came from Zeta Reticuli!

A lot of people said it was a lie — that Betty dreamed it up after watching an old TV show called *The Outer Limits*. But why would she do that? She and Barney were just normal people. It wasn't like today, when everyone wants to be a freakin' celebrity and put their videos on YouTube.

And you know what else? Betty Hill was white, and her husband was black. That was a big deal back then, and maybe that's why they weren't taken seriously. I don't understand why anyone would get weirded out by that. I mean, we're all humans, right? Look at me. I'm normal. Well, at least on the outside. It's just freakin' skin color. I bet if aliens came down and started a war, we'd forget all about that stuff and turn into one big human family.

That reminds me of something else. There was another president named Ronald Reagan. My dad said he was in charge when there was something called the Cold War between the United States and Russia. It wasn't really a war, but both countries were secretly building weapons and stuff, just in case the other one attacked. That doesn't make a lot of sense. Anyway, one day, Ronald Reagan was talking about a meeting he had with the Russian president, and he said:

> Just think how easy his task and mine might be in these meetings that we held, if suddenly there was a threat to this world from some other species, from

another planet, outside in the universe. We'd forget all the little local differences that we have between our countries, and we would find out once and for all that we really are all human beings here on this Earth together.

See what I mean? You can see it for yourself on YouTube. The government knows all about this stuff.

They just don't want us to know.

CHAPTER SIX

WHEN DAD CAME HOME from work the next day, he set a date for our camping trip.

"*This* weekend?" I complained.

I had planned on working on my story and trying to level up in *EverCraft*.

He gave me one of those looks — the one where he just stares and seems to want to roll his eyes but thinks better of it.

"Need more family time," he said, a cold beer in his hand. "It'll do you good to get some fresh air in your lungs." He took a swig from the bottle. "Buck up, kiddo. It'll be fun. Don't forget your inhaler."

And then he burped.

"Great," I said. "Just terrific."

Sleeping on the hard ground with bugs and insects is not my idea of fun.

• • •

I only had two days of freedom before the camping trip, so I spent them writing. I also played *EverCraft* but didn't level up like I wanted to. I kept getting killed by goblins.

Well, since I've already shared some of the story, you might as well keep reading. You remember what happened last, don't you? Max was standing on a frozen lake, feeling guilty for his father's death. He saw a vision of some sort in the ice. It was a waving white flag with a black horse on it. The ice shattered under his weight and he fell in the lake, but made it out just in time. Finally, he headed home with his dog, Alix, his heart full of sorrow.

II

The Man in the Dusty Suit

Max's dad had been his best friend and they'd done everything together: playing video games, watching fantasy movies, and racing remote control cars in the alley behind their house.

"Way to go, Little Prince," his dad would say whenever Max beat him at one of these games. But now, all that was gone.

He had pleaded with his dad for weeks to take him to see the acrobatic group Cirque du Soleil at the convention center. Finally, the date was set. His dad was leaving work early just for him. Max could barely contain his excitement and had visited the website every day for weeks, visions of high-wire stunts and contortionists dancing in his head. But they never saw the show. The accident changed everything.

The phone call came at five thirty, right before dinner. Max's mom had answered, and in one quick instant, a glass of water fell from her hands as if in slow motion, shattering on the checkered floor. She turned to Max, her expression blank.

"Your father," she whispered. "Max . . . no . . ."

After that Max ran. And kept running. He didn't know where he was going, but he ran as fast as he could and farther than he ever had before, Alix nipping and barking at his heels the whole while. The wind burned his cheeks and tears streamed down his face, but whether from the cold or someplace deep within, he didn't know. All he felt was . . . *numb.*

He had stepped onto the frozen lake as if in a trance, like something was drawing him there. And then came the vision — a black horse on a field of white.

His mom had made him talk to doctors, the school counselor. She even gave him books to read: *Coping with the Loss of a Parent, Grief and Its Stages,* but nothing seemed to help. He remembered sitting in the therapist's office, her voice distant and muffled, like someone underwater. For a long time he barely spoke, and when he did, his head was cast down.

He didn't know if he'd ever feel normal again.

Max woke up to the smell of bacon and eggs. He was ravenous. Downstairs, his mom looked at him like he was crazy as he shoveled food into his mouth.

"Good to see you're hungry," she said.

Max only continued to chomp down on his food. For some reason, he felt like he hadn't eaten in days.

After breakfast, he decided to go to the Botanical Gardens, one of his favorite places. He and his dad used to spend hours inside the damp and humid conservatory, studying the miniature trees and their small, twisting limbs that reached for the sky. Other times they walked through the English Garden and surveyed the colorful, rare flowers and amazing orchids.

But today, he and Alix were outside on the wide green lawn, which stretched out in front of him like a carpet. People were everywhere: lanky teenagers sprawled on the grass, and older gray-haired couples walked hand in hand among the flower beds.

Max threw a ratty tennis ball, and Alix retrieved it, her tail whipping back and forth like a wind-up toy. But as he bent down to pick up the ball, he noticed one man who stood out from the rest of the crowd. He was about twenty feet away, by the algae-covered water fountain. His skin was deathly white, like he'd never seen the sun, and his old-fashioned suit was black and dusty. The points of his shoes curled up at the end like party whistles.

Max froze as the man took a step forward.

Alix backed up, a fierce growl in her throat.

The strange figure opened his mouth in a grimace, a smear of red across a pale face. Max shivered.

Run! This way!

Max looked left, then right. *Who said that?*

He glanced down at Alix, tense and on edge.

Now, Max! Follow me!

What the . . . ? he thought, and took off after Alix as she sprinted toward the brick archway that led out of the park and into the surrounding woods.

A clap of thunder echoed across the park. Rain clouds loomed overhead like big, black pillows.

Max turned for a brief second and looked back.

He swallowed a gasp.

The man was floating in midair, his feet hovering a few inches above the ground. A dense cloud charged with lightning pulsated behind him.

No! Max screamed silently. *This isn't real!*

People everywhere fled for shelter, umbrellas popping open like a field of black flowers, but strangest of all, no one seemed to notice the weird figure gaining on him.

Max followed Alix into the forest. Rain crashed down.

Low-hanging tree branches scratched his face, but he kept moving forward, a freight train pounding in his chest.

Up ahead, the forest thinned to reveal a construction site enclosed by a chain-link fence. The metal links along the bottom were loose, making a space big enough for him to crawl through. Alix headed for the opening, dropped to her belly and scrambled through in one quick motion.

Max followed on his knees and elbows, the jagged points of the fence ripping his jacket.

He stood up and peered around, his breath coming in short bursts. Massive iron beams were stacked like cords of firewood on every side of the yard. Alix rested on her hind legs, panting furiously. Max looked past the fence, into the woods. There was no sign of the terrible man.

Now we're safe.

It was the voice again.

And it was coming from his dog.

"How?" Max stuttered, looking at Alix. "How did you —"

Something's after you, Max, she said. *Something . . . evil.*

So what do you think? I might try to get it published when I finish it. I read about one kid who sold his fantasy book to a big New York publisher and it became a bestseller. He was only sixteen. If he can do it, maybe I can too.

You never know, right?

CHAPTER SEVEN

"SIMON!"

Dad's voice boomed through the door.

Today was the day.

The family camping trip.

Great.

"Up and at 'em! Ten hut!"

I pulled the covers over my head. Dad always said stuff like that, like he was a drill instructor and I was a lowly recruit — a *plebe*, he called it.

I really didn't want to go. Maybe I could get sick all of a sudden — like one of those summer colds Mom always comes down with. She'd know I was faking it, though. She'd take my temperature, feel under my arms, and do all the other gross things moms do.

"Simon!" Dad's voice thundered again. "I said *now!*"

Ugh.

There was no getting around it. I climbed out of bed and prepared for the worst.

Even though Dad woke me up early, we didn't leave until late afternoon. He was down in the basement hammering and sawing stuff, making a bunch of noise. It was ridiculous. *Why'd he make me get up so early if we weren't leaving in the morning?* Mom was at the grocery store and then she was going to run some other errands.

Finally, after Mom came back and me and Dad loaded stuff in the car, we set out.

The campsite Dad chose was at Cape Henlopen State Park, about an hour from the Air Force base. I'd heard of it before but we'd never been there. I was glad we weren't staying at Murderkill River or Slaughter Beach. *Who'd want to camp at Slaughter Beach?*

There are all kinds of weird names around here for parks and beaches. There's even a place called Blades. *Blades.* How nice. If you camp there, you'll get cut up and buried in the woods. I don't know where these strange names came from. People have stories about them, but no one knows for sure. The only thing I'm sure about is that it creeps me out.

I sat in the back seat while Dad's giant SUV rumbled along the road. Loud rock music blared from the speakers. That's the only kind of music he likes. He plays the same two

CDs over and over. I think it's what he listened to when he was growing up. One time we were all in the car and Mom turned the radio to a classical music station before we started driving. Dad screwed up his face and looked at her. "Who listens to that kind of stuff?" he asked. "If I wanted to fall asleep, I would've stayed home."

Mom caved, and Dad put his old rock songs back on. I wished she wouldn't give in to him so much. I liked the little bit of classical music I'd heard. It made me think of fantasy books and deep forests and majestic mountains. But that all disappeared once a screeching guitar solo started blasting through the speakers.

After we left the Air Force base, Dad pulled off the highway and took what he called the scenic route. We passed gun shops, little churches, and old gas stations that seemed like they were frozen in time. Just about every house we went by had a pickup truck parked in front of it.

Mom wanted to stop in Rehoboth Beach for some saltwater taffy. A bunch of stores on the boardwalk sold it, but she had to have it from one special place. It was her favorite candy. All of her friends knew that if they went to Rehoboth they'd better bring back some taffy. I didn't really like taffy. It always got stuck in my teeth.

Dad couldn't find a place to park near the boardwalk, so he let me and Mom out and we walked to the shop. The boardwalk was packed like a can of sardines. Down on the beach, people in bathing suits were clumped together so tightly it was ridiculous. I mean, they were all right next to each other, with hardly any distance between them. That couldn't have been fun.

Mom was looking at all of the flavors of taffy. "Hmm," she murmured. "I'll take a box of the strawberry and a box of peppermint."

The girl behind the counter smiled and filled her order. Seagulls soared overhead, squawking and flapping their wings.

Mom opened one of the boxes as we walked back to the car. "Sure you don't want some?" she asked.

"I'm okay," I answered.

She popped a piece of taffy in her mouth and chewed. "I know you're not really looking forward to this, Simon," she said. "But your dad has wanted to do something as a family for a while. So try to remember that. Okay, sweetheart?"

"Yeah," I said. "I guess so."

We got to the campsite pretty quickly. Dad parked the SUV, then went inside a little office. He came back out a few minutes later with a red folder and gave us a thumbs-up.

"What's that?" I asked, pointing to the folder.

"Just safety regulations. Can never be too careful in the woods."

Even though this was Dad's Big Adventure, it wasn't *real* camping. It was one of those campgrounds where people get an assigned spot to pitch a tent. If anything goes wrong or you need to use the bathroom or get a soda, it's just a short walk away. But I couldn't tell Dad that. He thought he was roughing it. He even had a buck knife strapped to his belt.

He led us to a place in the woods not too far from the parking lot, where we set up the tent, a spiderlike contraption of unfolding poles and ropes. I hammered the stakes into the soft ground pretty easily, and Dad gave me an approving grin. I guess I was being manly. He liked that. He's big and tough, with huge muscles in his arms and legs. His calves are like split cantaloupes. Mom isn't much taller than me. She has nice brown eyes and a sharp nose — the same nose I have, people say. She told me one time that she really wanted to be an artist, but after she married Dad and had me, she didn't paint or draw as much as she used to. That made me feel bad.

Dad says she babies me too much, but she doesn't listen. She's always there for me, no matter what the problem. When I was really little, I asked Mom why she was black and Dad was white. She said that everyone was the same on the inside, and that they only learned to hate each other when they grew up. She said that she liked the military because there were so many mixed families: black and white, white and Asian, and all kinds of other combinations. I guess that's one thing I like about living on an Air Force base — we're all just one big family.

There was only one time when I had a problem. Well, other

than the time Jeremy Colbert called me a black nerd. But that didn't bother me. Grown-up nerds are cool. They invent computer games and make movies and write fantasy and sci-fi books. I saw a shirt on the Internet one time that had BLACK NERDS UNITE printed on the front, and I thought about buying it. In the end, I figured I didn't want the attention.

Anyway, there was this girl in school named Giselle who called me a half-breed. I didn't know what she meant, because I'd never heard the term before. So I came home and asked Mom about it. She said the girl probably didn't understand what she was saying. The next morning, Mom drove me to school and then went to talk to the principal. A week later, we had a special day in class where this lady visited and talked about racism and why it was bad. And you know what? Giselle said she was sorry, and we became friends for a while. She was pretty nice, actually. She said she'd heard those words in a movie, and that she'd never use them again. I think if grownups talked about this kind of stuff more, then maybe there wouldn't be so much hate in the world.

Mom brought what looked like the whole refrigerator in a couple of giant coolers. There were bologna sandwiches, ground beef for burgers, potato salad, steaks, some leftover roast chicken, and all kinds of other stuff. She even brought some of her special tomato soup so we could put it in a metal pot and warm it up over the fire. Dad brought beer.

After we set everything up and Mom had sprayed all of us with bug spray — which I hated — Dad cracked a beer and stood back and admired the tent. "That right there is an official Modular Command Post System tent," he announced. He took a swig from the bottle. "Also known as an MCPS. Sleeps four comfortably and also doubles as a disaster relief and emergency shelter."

And that's when I realized it.

I'd be sleeping with them.

My parents.

All of us.

In the same tent.

I looked to Mom, and she raised an eyebrow, like she was making fun of Dad. He walked away and rummaged around in a big green canvas bag, then pulled out a small bundle. He unfolded it. It was another tent, a smaller one. "Think this'll work for you, buddy?" he asked, holding it up.

"Yeah," I said, surprised.

Mom smiled.

The tent was camouflage green, with mosquito netting and a zipper up the front. Actually, I thought it was pretty cool. I could imagine hanging out in there all day playing video games and reading books. But I didn't think that would fly with Dad. He'd probably make me do pushups or go hiking or something. *What's the point of hiking, anyway? I don't understand it.*

Dad got the fire going—but not before delivering a safety lecture first—and then we all sat back in our lawn chairs. Gray clouds moved across the sky. It looked like rain. I watched the twigs and branches sizzle and pop. Tiny wisps of smoke rose into the air, and fireflies winked in and out of sight. It was already starting to get a little dark, and the rain clouds didn't help.

"See, Simon?" Mom said. "This is nice, isn't it?"

She was right. It wasn't that bad. In fact, I kind of liked it. I even wore the safari hat she bought me.

I pulled a book out of my backpack. Hopefully, I'd be able to read for a while before it got really dark. I'd brought a whole bunch of books because sometimes you start one but don't like it right away, and then want another one. This book was called *The White Hart of Eldridge*, and it was about this magical stag that could talk. I plucked out the bookmark.

"Simon," Dad said. "Go get some firewood."

I sighed. He was stretched out in a folding recliner, the kind made from that weird green material that looks like Velcro. It had built-in beer holders on each armrest. It was nuts. I remember when he bought it online. He spent a month making notes and comparing features on different chairs, like he was buying a freakin' car or something.

Mom tightened her lips, but Dad shot her a look. "He can do it," he declared, and waved his big hand lazily around the campsite. "Just stay close."

I put the book down on the ground and stood up. "Take the bucket," Dad added, nodding his head.

"Don't go far," Mom said. Dad rolled his eyes and took another swig of beer.

I picked up the military-green metal bucket from the ground and walked into the trees. A crusty old grill where people had lit barbecues was next to our campsite. *Who'd want to put their food on something like that, after a thousand people had used it?*

The moon was just coming out, peeking beneath bluish-black clouds. The air smelled like sap and pine. A row of white and tan RVs was parked along a dirt road off to the left. I bent down and grabbed a handful of broken branches and threw them in the bucket. I heard people laughing and talking from nearby campsites. Their voices drifted through the trees and echoed around me. It seemed to be getting darker by the second, like black ink spreading down, down, down to Earth.

There was a worn dirt path leading away from the site and I took it, scanning the ground for branches and small twigs. I imagined myself as Max Hollyoak, walking through the forest on my way to meet up with my companions. The battle would be coming soon. We'd fight the Darkling King and his evil minions. I'd lead the charge on my black horse, Nightmare, my flaming sword held high.

One spot in the trees ahead of me looked brighter than

everything around it. Not like super bright, but kind of glowing. It wasn't a campfire. At first I thought it was moonlight, but when I looked up, the moon was way too high. Its light wasn't strong enough.

There it was again —

a flash —

like in a movie when a spy holds up a piece of glass to signal another spy. It was like that, but the light was bigger. Then it was pulsing.

That's weird.

Goose bumps rose on my arms, even though the air was humid. A few gnats buzzed around my head. A thought crawled its way to the front of my brain. I didn't want to think about it. About *them*. But I couldn't help myself.

I kept moving forward. Branches snapped under my sneakers. I heard someone playing a guitar far away, their voice wobbling on the air.

Hoo hoo.

I whipped my head around.

That sounded like an owl.

But I didn't see anything.

Hoo hoo.

I turned back around and looked up. It was in the tree above me, looking down, its huge eyes gazing at me. I froze. *Just an owl,* I thought, but then . . .

QUIET. REMAIN STILL.

The voice rang inside my head like a command.

I felt a buzz, like electricity on my skin. I dropped the bucket. The ground spun beneath me. The owl was suddenly too close. *How did it get out of the tree so fast?*

Its eyes were pressed up against my forehead. I swung my arms, trying to beat it away. "Help!" I cried out. "Mom!"

The world tilted.

And then everything went black.

CHAPTER EIGHT

"SIMON. WAKE UP! Wake up, Simon!"

A stick was poking me in the back. Mom leaned over me, and Dad knelt by her side. "What happened, son? You have an asthma attack?"

Mom felt my forehead. "Simon. Where's your inhaler?"

I patted my pocket. It was there, but I didn't remember using it.

"What happened?" Dad asked again.

I sat up on my elbows and looked left, then right. I was dizzy. The forest was nearly dark. I heard crickets chirping.

"Just get him back to the tent," Mom said. "C'mon, Simon. Let's get up."

Dad said I was gone for fifteen minutes before they came looking for me. They found me lying face-down under broken branches. "I was just collecting wood," I said. "And then I saw a light. I felt tired. That's all I remember."

"Light?" Mom ventured.

"Yeah, like moonlight, but different. Brighter. And there was an owl."

"An owl?" they both echoed.

I didn't sleep at all that night. Mom asked me if I wanted to stay in their tent, but I said I'd be okay on my own. I didn't want to look like a big baby. To tell you the truth, though, I was afraid.

The whole night I heard creaks and calls from the wild, and little creatures scratching at the tent. Rain drummed the canvas roof, and the fabric flapped in the wind every few minutes.

What had happened?

And then I remembered:

QUIET. REMAIN STILL.

A shock went through me — a tingling all over my body.

Did I hear that voice, or was it in my imagination?

I rolled over on my side and tried to go to sleep. I didn't want to think about it.

But have you ever tried to not think about something? It's impossible.

I picked up *The White Hart of Eldridge* and used a flashlight to read a few pages, but I couldn't concentrate. I was agitated. The slightest sound made me jump. People were laughing in the distance. I heard the guitar playing again, and some guy singing. Actually, his voice wasn't bad, and I thought for a moment it'd put me to sleep, because it was kind of a soft and dreamy song, but the moment was broken when I got an itch all of a sudden. It felt like a spider bite, right on my stomach.

I had to see what it was.

I sat up and reached for the flashlight, then pulled my shirt up and shined it on my stomach.

My heart flopped in my chest.

I tried to swallow, but my tongue felt like it was too big.

No.

No.

It was a mark. A scoop mark, like a piece of skin had been plucked right out of me.

I knew what it was.

I had been abducted.

The Grays had been right here in this campground.

And now I had an implant inside of me.

CHAPTER NINE

I WOKE UP to the smell of bacon.

Where was I?

This wasn't my room.

I was sleeping on something hard and uneven. Birds were chirping.

And then it all came flooding back.

We were camping.

Something in the woods . . .

The light . . . the owl . . . the scoop mark . . .

I looked down at my stomach. It was still there, a little hole about the size of a pencil eraser. Tiny red bumps were around it, but there wasn't any blood. I ran my fingers across it. Definitely an implant. I could feel something under the hole, hard and irritating, like when a pebble gets stuck in your shoe.

I sat up.

Why? Why me?

My hands went clammy, and my heart started thumping. I rummaged around in my backpack and found my inhaler. I pressed the pump and felt the cool mist hit the back of my throat. *One ... two ... three ... exhale.*

My breathing returned to normal. I sat there for a moment before unzipping the flap and stepping outside. The bright sunlight made me squint. A frying pan sat over a bed of glowing coals. The bacon grease crackled and hissed. Everything was green and hazy.

"There he is," Mom said.

She and Dad were sitting near the fire pit in their lawn chairs sipping coffee. Dad's eyes were red, and he had a bunch of beard stubble. Mom had on shorts and no makeup, and her hair was messy. I'd never seen her look like that before. She usually looked really pretty. Dad called her Sugar Mama and she called him Big Bear. It made me want to barf.

Should I tell them?

No. I couldn't. They'd think I was crazy.

But it happened. I *knew* it happened.

"Feeling better, trouper?" Dad asked. "Want some bacon?"

I didn't want bacon.

I took a few steps and flopped down into my chair. Mom got up and put a hand on my forehead. "How are you feeling?"

"Okay," I mumbled. But I wasn't. I felt totally wiped out.

She frowned. "Let me get you some juice."

Mom got up and opened one of the coolers a few feet away. Dad looked at me for a long time. I felt his eyes on me. Judging me, like always. "Weather report said there was lightning last night," he started. "I think I saw a few flashes when you went off to get wood." He shifted in his seat. "Now, I was thinking, maybe it was lightning you saw. Hell, maybe you even got struck."

Mom handed me a paper cup full of orange juice. I took a sip.

She made a thoughtful face. "Do you remember seeing any lightning, Simon?"

No, Mom. It was aliens. The Grays.

"No," I answered. "Just an owl."

There was silence for a minute. The smell of the bacon suddenly made me feel sick. My stomach was churning. "Yeah," I said, and my voice sounded far away, like it wasn't really coming from me. "I felt like an owl attacked me."

"An owl?" Dad laughed. "What the hell's an owl got to do with anything? Owls don't attack people, Simon."

Mom shot him a look. "*Bill.*"

"Well, maybe it was heat exhaustion," Dad said. "You know, with your asthma and everything."

I felt like shouting. I passed out in the woods and Dad didn't even seem to get it. *I had an implant inside of me!*

I took a breath. "I want to go home," I said. "I don't feel good."

Dad sighed. "First lesson of camping, Simon. Don't wimp out."

Mom looked at Dad, and it was a look I knew well, because she used it on me all the time. "I think we should get Simon home," she said, staring directly at him.

It wasn't a suggestion.

Dad sighed again and shook his head. "Pitiful," I heard him mutter under his breath. "Damn pitiful."

CHAPTER TEN

THE MOTION OF the car made me fall asleep in the back seat. I had a dream that I was lost in the woods. I was running, but I didn't know from what. Tree branches scratched my face as I ran, but I couldn't stop. Something was after me . . . something terrible . . . something with spindly arms and legs and almond-shaped eyes . . .

"Simon."

"Simon."

I opened my eyes.

"We're home, honey," Mom said, feeling my forehead again. "You're burning up."

They helped me out of the car, and I went straight to my room. Mom brought me some hot milk. I don't know what hot milk is supposed to do for you, but people drink it in movies all the time. If you live in England, people drink tea when something's wrong.

After I drank the milk and Mom had left the room, I got on the Internet.

It was a mistake.

I typed "alien scoop marks," and what I found was terrible.

There were pictures.

Pictures of people whose skin had been punctured by instruments of the aliens.

There were photos of men, women, and children — all of them showing the little marks. There was saggy skin, white skin, black skin, hard-muscled skin, loose, flabby skin. All kinds. There were pictures of implants under the skin in people's ears, arms, legs — even their noses. It was awful. I felt like I was going to be sick. My heart started racing.

Breathe . . .

Breathe . . .

I lifted my shirt and looked again. It hadn't changed. It was red and sore, and felt like a bee sting.

I shut down the computer. If I kept looking, I wouldn't be able to sleep later tonight. One time I stayed up all night with the lights on after watching a special on the Discovery Channel all about the Grays. One of the people on the show said that they didn't come from another planet, but from another *dimension.* That really creeped me out. There could be other dimensions all around us, and we wouldn't even know it. Other people thought they were fallen angels. *Demons.* They said just thinking about them could make them appear. And if that wasn't bad enough, they fed on fear. Great. They could also float you right out of your bed in the middle of the night. And they could put you in a trance just by looking at you.

I stared at my empty milk glass. Sunshine came down in diagonal rays through the window. How could it be so beautiful outside after what had just happened to me?

I stayed in my room for most of the day, but I couldn't concentrate on video games or my Max Hollyoak story. I didn't eat hardly anything at dinner. Every creak and groan in the house startled me.

When I finally went to bed, I took out the unicorn nightlight Mom got for me when I was little and plugged it in. I picked up a book called *The Swords of GlimmerLand* from my shelf. It was a fantasy about a kid who discovers he's a king in another land. He has to travel there by dreams. It usually helps me fall asleep, but not that night.

I was thinking about them.

Over the next two days, Mom kept asking me if I was okay. She felt my forehead, took my temperature, and fussed over me like I was a baby. She even made grilled cheese sandwiches and tomato soup, my favorite. I felt disconnected, like I was wearing someone else's skin. I can't really explain it. It was like

I wasn't really me. I only felt half visible. Maybe the other half of me was still back there in the woods.

Mom didn't understand it. "You don't have a fever anymore," she said. "And you're not achy?"

"No," I answered. "I'm fine, Mom."

She gave me the Mom look, and then set a plate of scrambled eggs in front of me. "Maybe it's a tick bite," she offered. "You know, Lyme disease? If you're not better soon, I'll take you to see Dr. Martens."

I didn't want to see Dr. Martens. He had bad breath. I had my tonsils taken out last year, and he was the one who did it. I got to eat ice cream for a week, though. That was the only good thing about it.

"A tick bite wouldn't make me pass out," I said quietly.

I don't know if she heard me, because she was already washing the pan that the eggs were in.

I finished my breakfast and went back upstairs.

I made a promise to myself to not look up stuff on the Internet, no matter what.

And then I looked up stuff on the Internet.

I looked at pictures of cows cut open by the aliens. A doctor said the cut marks were precise and clean, like some kind of laser had made the incision. Their hearts and lungs were missing. It was awful, but I couldn't stop myself.

I read about a woman who said she'd been taken by the Grays from the time she was a little girl. They first came for her when she was four years old. She was playing in her room when they suddenly appeared. They wanted to study her, and do some tests. She called them the "little men with the black eyes."

That really creeped me out.

I shut down the computer again.

I needed to do something to get my mind off aliens. Tony Deaver and I used to take our bikes down to this place called Dead Man's Hill and race to the bottom. We weren't supposed to. It was dangerous, and there were signs all around it that said so:

DANGER. CAUTION. NO BICYCLES.

They put the signs up after a kid named Stevie Chase broke his collarbone zooming down the hill. That didn't keep anybody away, though. It just made more people want to go there. I thought about going, but then it hit me.

Dead Man's Hill was in the woods.

I didn't want to be in the woods again, even in the bright sunshine. There were lots of reports of people being abducted in the woods. There was this one guy named Travis Walton who was taken and kept for days by the Grays. He wrote a book about it called *Fire in the Sky.*

I went out to the garage and got my bike. Mom and Dad bought it for me last year when I turned twelve. They actually let me pick it out online. It was a mountain bike, with fat, chunky tires that were good for dirt paths. I didn't think I'd be riding up any mountains, but it looked cool.

The sun felt good on my skin as I pedaled down the street. The sky was a brilliant blue. Remember when I said there are rules on the base? Well, if you're caught riding a bike on the sidewalk, you can get a fine.

I passed all the cookie-cutter houses, each one with a ticking sprinkler. For some reason, that made me think of fall, because summer was always too short. Dad forces me to rake leaves in the fall. That's one chore that just doesn't make sense. I wonder what would happen if someone let leaves pile up on their lawn. I mean, they're *leaves*. They're *supposed* to fall from trees. I'm sure they serve some kind of purpose, like, eventually, they return to the earth or something. After raking them, we have to put them in big lawn bags and then a military truck comes by and picks them up. We even have to use certain *types* of bags. It's ridiculous.

I turned a corner onto Mockingbird Lane, where Tony Deaver lives. A car pulled onto the road from the opposite direction. I stopped pedaling. That wasn't right. It was a one-way street. The car just came out of nowhere. It was long and black, and as it passed me, I turned to look. The driver wore a black hat, just like the ones I'd seen in Mom's old Humphrey Bogart movies. His skin was waxy and white. My blood went cold.

He was looking right at me.

CHAPTER ELEVEN

I **KNEW WHAT** I'd just seen, but didn't want to admit it. There was no doubt.

He was an MIB: a Man in Black.

No one knew who they were or where they came from, but one thing was sure. Every time a person got abducted, a Man in Black showed up shortly after. There was even a movie about them, but it was all a bunch of comedy stuff.

I rushed into my room and opened up my laptop. My fingers hovered over the keys. "No," I said. "I won't do it."

But then I did it anyway.

From the Journal of UFO Research:

MIBs, or Men in Black, are a strange phenomenon associated with alleged alien abductions. Abductees often report being visited by one or more of these entities shortly after experiencing an encounter. They are often described as tall and menacing, dressed in basic black clothing, sometimes appearing as if they are from another decade, the 1950s in particular.

Some have speculated that they are government time travelers, sent to warn experiencers to keep quiet about their alleged abductions. Others say that they are working with the aliens in a mass hypnosis project.

I shut down the computer.

First the implant and now a Man in Black? Could it all be in my head?

It couldn't be. There was no way I imagined all this stuff.

And then it dawned on me.

They were going to come back.

The Grays didn't just abduct you once and then leave you alone. They came back for you, and checked whatever they did to you the first time.

I was doomed. Being monitored. And there was nothing I could do about it.

I spent part of the next day in the backyard playing with a remote-controlled car I'd gotten for Christmas. I was trying to do something regular. Something *normal*. Something that wouldn't draw the aliens to me.

They fed on fear.

So I couldn't be afraid. That is when they appear.

I shook my head and focused on the car. Actually, it wasn't a car, it was more like one of those monster truck things. When I first got it, I took it into the woods and maneuvered it around little dirt mountains and rock piles. It was kind of fun, but it got boring pretty fast, so I stowed it away with all my other abandoned toys.

After playing mindlessly with the car for a while, I moped around in my room. I stayed away from the Internet because I didn't want to get lured into looking up alien stuff.

Mom had given up on trying to get me out of the house. She couldn't even convince me to go to the art supply store with her, which is something I usually like to do. She paints these little watercolors that are about the size of a baseball card. They're all over the house. Most of them are nature scenes, but there are a few of me and Dad. I mean, they don't *look* like me or Dad, but that's not the point, right? It's just something she likes to do.

When she got back, I told her I was feeling better, and tried to look as normal as possible. I even gave her a fake smile. I really didn't want to go to the doctor's. "Good," she said. "Maybe you just got overheated or something." She put her hand on my forehead for the ten-thousandth time. I blew a breath through my nose. "Okay, well, you're probably due for a physical anyway, so we should still make an appointment."

Great. I'd have to cough and get a flashlight pointed in my eyes and open my mouth wide and say "ahhhh" and a bunch of other dumb stuff.

I went up to my room and finally gave in to the lure of *EverCraft*, but died about a thousand times and lost two levels.

The smell of meatloaf drifted up the stairs. I like Mom's meatloaf. It's one of my favorites. Unfortunately, I had a nervous stomach and wasn't hungry. I was thinking about the Man in Black and his waxy face. But I had to go downstairs sooner or later. I was surprised they hadn't called me yet.

I took the steps one at a time and quietly walked into the dining room.

"There he is," Dad said.

Mom turned and looked at me.

"Still feeling okay, honey?"

"Yeah," I lied. "Yes."

"Good," Dad said. "You'll be back to normal in no time."

The next five minutes felt like I was in some kind of time warp, like I'd been sitting at the table for hours. Dad was talking to Mom about some dumb TV show, and she didn't seem the least bit interested. She just smiled and nodded along, like Dad was the funniest guy in the world. I wish she wouldn't do that.

Dad finally stopped talking and looked at me. "Thought Mom's meatloaf was your favorite, buddy."

I stared at my plate. I had barely touched my food. The gravy on the potatoes was cold and looked like a puddle of gloop.

Mom frowned. "Can you manage a few vegetables?"

I speared a Brussels sprout with my fork. "Do you think there are aliens?" I asked.

It just came out all of a sudden. I didn't even have time to think about it. Maybe deep down inside I *wanted* to tell them. Whatever. Too late now.

Dad looked at Mom and then sighed.

"Simon," Dad said, "have you been reading those books again?"

"No," I said. "That night. In the woods . . ."

Mom leaned across the table. She put her hand over mine. "What happened? Do you remember?"

Dad got up and opened the refrigerator. He pulled out a beer bottle and twisted off the top, then sat down again. "What do you think you saw, Simon?"

I looked up from my plate. Mom squeezed my hand. "You can tell us, honey."

I let out a breath. "I . . . I was just walking. I saw a light in the woods, and then it seemed like an owl was looking at me. I heard a voice. It said to stay silent and not to move. That's the last thing I remember."

I felt like a giant weight had just come off my chest. Dad looked at Mom and shook his head. Nobody said anything. All I could hear was the hum of the refrigerator and the *tick-tick-tick* of the sprinkler outside.

"And you think this was . . . an alien voice?" Mom finally asked. She said it hesitantly, like she wasn't sure she was asking the right question, or using the proper terminology.

I looked up. "Yes. I think it was one of the gray aliens."

"Simon," Dad said, and his voice was calm and concerned, a tone I never heard from him. "I know those books scared you when you were little, but you're almost thirteen now. There's no such thing as aliens. If there were, the Air Force would've told us about it. I would know, son."

"What about Roswell?" I asked. "Aliens came there a long time ago, and the government tried to cover it up."

"It's all make-believe," Mom said. "Like people saying they saw Elvis at the local gas station."

"Who's Elvis?"

Dad blew out a breath through his nostrils. "What your mom is trying to say, son, is that the Internet has all kinds of things on it that aren't true. People like to make up stories because crazy people will believe them."

"So you're saying I'm crazy?"

Dad swallowed. He shifted in his seat. "No. I'm just saying you can't believe everything you read."

I stood up. "Well, what about this, then?"

I pulled my shirt up and pointed to the little hole in my stomach.

"What the hell is that?" Dad asked, leaning in.

Mom squinted. "I was right," she said quietly. "You *were* bitten by a tick."

"It's not a tick," I said.

"Well, what is it, then?" Mom asked.

"It's an implant," I told them. "And it was put there by aliens."

CHAPTER TWELVE

MOM CLOSED HER eyes and then opened them again slowly. Dad stared at his beer bottle.

I'd done it.

I told them about aliens.

What were they going to do now?

"Simon," Dad started, "this has to stop. Aliens aren't real. You have to put an end to this right now."

I raged inside. He didn't know. He didn't know anything. The Man in Black could be out there right now, driving slowly around the block in his long car, waiting for the lights to go out in my room.

Was he going to come to the house?

Knock on the door in the middle of the night?

Mom let out a long breath. "Honey, I think we have to see Dr. Martens. Whatever that is on your skin should be looked at. It must've happened in the woods."

"No!" I shouted. "It's real!"

Silence filled the kitchen. My head was ringing. I'd just shouted at my parents.

"Go up to your room, Simon," Dad ordered me, and his voice had a hard edge to it. "We do not shout in this house."

Right. Who'd he think he was kidding? He shouted at Mom all the time.

I scooted my chair back, scraping its legs across the linoleum floor, and headed up the steps.

I lay back on the bed and picked up *The White Hart of Eldridge.* I read for about ten minutes, trying to make my brain connect to the words on the page, but after a while, I realized I wasn't even paying attention.

Why did I do it? Why did I just blurt it out?

I didn't even mean to. It just kind of happened all of a sudden.

I turned over on my side and tried to read again.

"The White Hart was here," said Tomas, kneeling down to look at the tracks.

"Are you certain?" King Aelfwane replied. "It seems that her tracks are magical, and can change appearance depending on the phase of the moon. Just yesterday, Maeve said she saw the tracks of a great bear."

Tomas stood up. "I am certain," he said. "Maeve said the stag spoke to her in a dream. She said . . .

I woke up with a dry mouth.

I was so thirsty. Soft light was pouring through the window. Moonlight?

But moonlight wouldn't spill over my old action figures on the windowsill and then down to the floor like that. It was more than just light — it looked like the mist they used in the hospital when I had the asthma attack.

I felt awake but asleep at the same time.

The little hairs on my arms were standing up, like there was some kind of static electricity in the room.

A scuffling sound outside my window made my heart jump. I tried to get up, and that's when I knew something was really wrong.

I couldn't move.

I tried to open my mouth, but it was locked shut.

No! I screamed inside my head. Mom!

But no one heard me.

I strained to move my toes, my arms. Nothing.

Something stirred in the darkness. I saw it out of the corner of my eye. I wanted to focus on it, but my head hurt. It took every ounce of strength to move just the tiniest bit, and when I did, it disappeared.

But now I saw it.

A small orb of light appeared in the darkest corner of the room.

I wanted to pull the covers up over my face, but my arms were lifeless.

It rose from the floor and moved toward me.

It was getting closer, bigger.

But then I realized that it wasn't just a light. It was being held up by something. Something that suddenly appeared in the deeper shade of black around it.

It was a body. A small figure, with a long, skinny hand and four fingers.

Blinding light struck my head.

I woke up lying on a cold metal slab. The walls were white and curved, a long tube, fading into shadow. There was a sound, like the whirring of machines. I tried to lift my arm, but it felt as if it weighed ten thousand pounds. My breath was coming fast and short. I was having an attack! I needed my inhaler!

And then I saw them.

Three gray aliens appeared out of thin air, like they just came right out of the walls.

They walked toward me. No! *I tried to shout.* Stay away! *But my mouth didn't open.*

I couldn't turn my head, but rolled my eye to the left. A long needle and some other instruments were set on a tray. One of the aliens picked up a shiny silver tool and started scraping skin from my arm. My heart thundered in my chest. He put the shavings in a little glass bottle and handed it to another alien, who walked away.

Then one of the tallest ones leaned over me and stared into my eyes. I tried to look away, but he wouldn't let me. I thought I was going to die.

Mom! *I wailed inside my head.* Dad!

But no sound left my lips. I smelled something — something damp and musty, like mushrooms kept in the refrigerator too long. The alien's eyes were so black it was like looking into a jar of ink, wet and glossy. It blinked slowly, like a weird lizard or something.

My heartbeat slowed down. **REMAIN CALM,** *I heard inside my head. It was communicating with me, just like before. I tried to focus on the alien's face. It was one I had seen thousands of times in books and movies, but now I was seeing it for real. It was real!*

It was all real!

The way it moved made me think of a praying mantis — like a big insect. Its skin was almost see-through — the nose, just two tiny pinpricks; the mouth, nothing but an expressionless grim line.

It cocked its head, like it was trying to understand me. The next thing I knew, a bunch of cold hands turned me over. They were pressing on my back, almost as if they were counting the vertebrae in my spine. It felt like being bitten by mosquitoes.

There was nothing I could do.

I was helpless.

I woke up.

I was still in the curved white room. I tried to see if I was in a spaceship, but there were no windows and nothing to focus on, just white walls and the whirring sound. Whir . . . whir . . . click . . . click . . .

A flash of light blinded me, flooding my brain with images: cave paintings of stick figures and animals, our solar system in the deep black of space, images of cities and cars and people all moving in a sped-up time-lapse sequence. I saw a mushroom cloud rising in the air, tree branches bent back from a ferocious wind, and a red sun that blazed like fire.

Then another image came. It was a night sky, full of stars.

NIBIRU, *I heard.*

They were speaking to me. I couldn't see them, but the voice was in my head.

NIBIRU.

I passed out again.

I woke up to blurry, hovering shapes. A gray alien was standing over me. He was the tallest one. The General, I called him in my head. He reached toward my mouth and opened it with long fingers. *No! Help! I tried to bite down — do anything that would stop this nightmare — but I couldn't.*

A soft, spongy sensation filled my throat. I wanted to retch, but there was nothing I could do.

They looked into my ears and nostrils.

They clipped my fingernails and cut a piece of my hair.

And then there was other stuff too. Stuff I can't tell you.

CHAPTER THIRTEEN

I **WOKE UP** to wet sheets.

No!

The last time I wet the bed was months ago!

Now it had happened again.

Why?

I didn't remember falling asleep, but *The White Hart of Eldridge* was lying on the floor. It must have slipped from my hands.

I got up and stripped the bed. Maybe Mom wouldn't notice. As soon as the thought came into my head, I knew it was ridiculous. Of course she'd notice. She's the one who does the freakin' laundry. Maybe she'd run an errand and I could use the washing machine. *But I didn't know how to use it.* I could figure it out, though, right? How hard could it be?

I put the wet sheets under the bed, then went into the bathroom and washed up. I looked at the little mark on my stomach and poked it with my finger. It felt the same, just a tiny little itch. *I could cut it out*, I suddenly thought. No. I couldn't. There'd be blood all over the place. Mom would freak out.

I told them, I suddenly remembered. *About the implant.*

I looked at my face in the mirror. It was all splotchy. My back was sore, and I had a headache. Plus, I felt like I'd just run twenty laps in gym class.

Why was I so tired?

Sure enough, Mom went out on one of her errands — a Ladies' Lunch, she called it — and I bolted up the stairs to get the sheets from under the bed. I had to wash them before she came back. I looked at the clock — 11:30. She'd definitely be gone for a while, but I didn't want to take any chances. I balled up the sheets in my arms and ran back downstairs.

The front door opened. I gulped.

"Simon? What are you doing?"

I froze — the wet sheets in my hands, my face turning hot. "I . . . I thought you left."

"I forgot my purse," she said, closing the door behind her and walking toward me. "What happened, Simon? What are you doing with those —"

"It happened again," I said, not even trying to hide it. I mean, I was standing there with balled-up wet sheets. "I didn't mean to, Mom."

And then I cried.

It just all came pouring out. I dropped the sheets, and she threw her arms around me. "It's okay, baby," she said, stroking my hair. "We're going to get you some help. This is too much, Simon. All this talk of aliens and stuff. You're making yourself sick."

I wanted her to stop — wanted to pull away and tell her I wasn't crazy — but I didn't. I just let her hold me like that for a long time, until my chest finally stopped heaving and I'd finished blubbering all over her nice dress.

PART TWO

CHAPTER FOURTEEN

THEY TOOK ME to the doctor.

That's what happens when you're a kid. Your parents can do anything they want, and you have no rights.

It wasn't Dr. Martens. It was another doctor.

"There's got to be a rational explanation," Dad had said, when Mom told him about "my incident."

"It has to stop, Simon," he'd said, using his military voice, the one where he narrows his eyes and flexes his jaw. "The bed-wetting and the alien talk. Do you understand?"

I didn't answer him. He was the one who didn't understand. He'd never understand.

The doctor was all booked up, so we had to wait a few days before I could get an appointment. I felt like a condemned man on the way to what they called "the gallows" in the old Western movies Dad watched.

I spent most of the time in my room. I couldn't concentrate on reading or writing so I watched some dumb fantasy movies on my computer instead. But they didn't hold my interest. I was tired all the time, and I didn't know why.

Was it the implant? Was it doing something to me? Downloading and sending my vital signs to the aliens' ship? And then there was the Man in Black. *How did he fit into all of this?*

Finally, the day came. Dad was at work, so Mom took me to the appointment. I sat in the front seat, and the cold air from the AC blasted onto my face. Mom looked over at me at every stoplight and touched my knee. "It's going to be all right, Simon," she tried to assure me. "We're gonna get this all figured out."

But it didn't help.

I was terrified.

The doctor's office was in the base hospital, in a special building away from all the regular sick people. They thought I had a different kind of sickness.

The one where you're sick in the head.

What was the doctor going to do? Run tests? Hook me up to a machine? Put me in the looney bin?

A man in a white uniform took us through a bunch of

long, cold hallways that reminded me of a maze. It seemed like I had been there before, but I knew I hadn't.

Finally, he led us into an office and I sat down while Mom went up to the receptionist. After a minute, she came over and took a seat next to me. She tried to hold my hand, but I pushed it away. That was for babies. I wasn't a baby.

I looked at every person that came in and tried to figure out what was wrong with them. They all looked normal, with their nice clothes and fake smiles. But they were damaged. On the inside. Like me.

We sat there for what seemed like forever, until a guy with a clipboard came loping in from around a corner. He reminded me of somebody you'd see in a commercial for shampoo, because his hair was so curly it was ridiculous. "Simon?" he called, looking around the room.

Me and Mom got up and followed Mr. Curly Hair down a hallway with frosted glass doors on both sides. He wore white shoes, and they squeaked on the polished floor. It drove me crazy. Each step he took echoed in the sterile white hallway and got under my skin.

He stopped in front of a door with a sign that read DR. CHARLOTTE CROSS.

"She'd like to see you first," the guy said quietly to Mom, opening the door. He then turned to me and leaned down a little, like I was a freakin' five-year-old. "She'll just be a min-ute, Simon," he whispered. "You can have a seat."

I hated when adults did that. Trying to act like they knew you when they didn't.

Mom disappeared, and I sat down in a green chair and stared at the white walls. My eyes drifted to a table next to me, stacked with all the latest celebrity magazines. *Who cares about this junk? Why would anybody read it?* I imagined all the hands that had thumbed through the pages, spreading germs.

I took out my phone and fiddled around with a game I'd downloaded a few weeks before. I couldn't get a signal, though, so I stuck it back in my pocket.

What was Mom saying to the doctor?

I didn't have to wait long, because a minute later she came through the door wearing a forced smile. "You'll like her," she said in an overeager way, like she was trying to convince me of something. She sat down and then stroked my hair. "Just be yourself, Simon, and try to talk to her. She wants to help, okay?"

I let out a frustrated breath. "Okay."

Dr. Cross had short blond hair and spoke with an accent. I think she was from England. Her office was cold and white, with hardly anything on the walls. She sat across from me in a black swivel chair, studying some paperwork.

I stared at my sneakers. I heard the ticking of the clock on her desk. The elevator door outside opening and then closing. The muffled voices in the office next to hers. I swallowed, and felt like the whole world could hear it.

"So, Simon," she finally said, looking up. "I'm glad you came to talk. That's a great first step."

She was messing with me. I knew how these people worked. They pretended to be your friend and then they put you on drugs.

She sat with her legs crossed. A pad and pencil were balanced on her lap. The ticking of the clock was as loud as fireworks.

Tick

Tick

Tick.

"So what do you want to know?" I finally asked.

"Well," she said, "let's start at the beginning."

So that's what I did.

I told her about the alien conspiracy, going all the way back to Roswell.

I told her about how the Grays broke the treaty on abducting people.

I told her about Betty and Barney Hill and Area 51 and everything else.

Finally, I told her about the camping trip, and how the

aliens put an implant inside of me. The whole time she just sat very still and nodded her head, every now and then writing something on her pad.

"Can you draw a picture of what the aliens look like?" she asked.

She ripped a piece of paper from her pad and handed it to me along with her pen. I set it on my knee and quickly sketched a gray alien. It looked like this:

I handed it to her. She cocked her head, but didn't say anything. She just scribbled something in her notepad and then placed the drawing in a folder on her desk.

"Thanks for telling me all this, Simon," she said. "You are very brave to do so."

"Is that it?" I asked.

"Just a few more questions," she said, and then glanced down at her notepad. She raised her head. "So, how's it going in school?"

I shrugged. "Okay."

She nodded. "Has anyone ever picked on you? Have you been a victim of bullying?"

"Coupla times," I mumbled.

"Did they assault you in any other way?"

What does she mean?

She shifted in her seat. "Touching," she said. "Did anyone touch you in an inappropriate manner?"

"No!" I raised my voice. *Is this what she thinks is going on?*

She cocked her head. "No teachers or students making you do something you didn't want to do?"

I shook my head. "No," I said again, more forcefully, drawing out the word.

"Okay, Simon," she said in a reassuring tone. "That's good. I promise we're going to make things better for you, okay? That's what I'm here for."

There was a moment of silence. I nodded without looking at her.

She wrote something else on her notepad. I really wanted

to know what it was. "Well," she said, "that's it for now. We'll see each other again soon. You can have a seat in the waiting room. Can you ask your mother to come back in for a moment? We won't be long."

I got up and felt sweat on the back of my shirt. I went out and told Mom the doctor wanted to see her again, then sat down and waited. It felt like the whole world was crashing all around me. *She thinks I'm being abused. Jeez.*

There was a kid sitting across from me with his mom, rocking back and forth while she stroked his hair. *Is that what I look like when Mom fiddles with my hair?* He was younger than me, maybe in sixth grade. He looked like a bird that had fallen out of its nest.

A few minutes later, Mom came back out, and we went home. I asked her what the doctor told her, and she said not to worry — there was some medicine they were going to give me to make everything better.

See?

Told you.

CHAPTER FIFTEEN

THEY GAVE ME PILLS. They were supposed to help with my "uncontrolled thoughts," Mom had said.

No one believed me.

Maybe I was crazy.

Mom kept the pills in her and Dad's bathroom. There were three different kinds, all with weird-sounding names I couldn't even pronounce. Mom told me Dr. Cross said it would take a while for all the medications to "stabilize."

She watched me swallow the pills with a glass of water and then made me open my mouth so she could check. That reminded me of a movie I saw once. It was rated R, and I wasn't supposed to watch it, but Mom and Dad weren't home, and I watched it anyway. There was a scene where a guy in prison had to take medicine every day, and the guards always made him open his mouth, move his tongue around, and tilt his head back. He ended up getting stabbed in a prison break. It was a pretty awful movie.

Being on the meds made me feel woozy. I was tired all the time, and my head hurt. Sometimes my legs and back ached, too. Other than that, I didn't feel any different. I still thought about what had happened — the camping trip and the Man in Black. I couldn't get it out of my head.

My friend Tony Deaver finally came back from Mexico, and I met him at the bowling alley, a place we liked hanging out. Well, not *inside* the bowling alley, but out by the bicycle rack.

"Hey, hombre," he said. "What you been up to?"

"Nothing," I said. "Just playing video games."

I wondered for a minute if I should tell him about the camping trip and the Man in Black. *He'd believe me, right?* I mean, we used to play lots of sci-fi and fantasy games. If anyone would believe me, he would. At least he'd be more open to it than some people — like Mom and Dad and Dr. Cross.

I leaned my bike up against the brick wall and sat down with my back resting against it. Tony did the same. The air was stuffy and the sun was blazing, casting long shadows between the bars of the bicycle rack.

"I saw a giant iguana in Mexico," Tony said, pulling out

his phone and scrolling through some photos. "Look at this, hombre."

I leaned over. A giant lizard with green scaly skin and huge eyes stared back at me. A shiver went up my spine. I turned away.

Tony sighed. "Dude, what is *wrong* with you? You're not even talking."

I studied my sneakers. "Something happened."

"You kissed Cathy Taylor?"

I smirked. "No."

Tony was always teasing me about a girl in our class named Cathy Taylor. She helped me with my homework one time, and Tony said she was giving me googly eyes, whatever that meant.

"I went camping with my mom and dad," I said.

"Really? Did you have to poop in the woods?"

"No."

"Did your dad shoot a rabbit and make you skin it?"

"No."

Tony frowned, crestfallen. "Well . . . did you eat a poisonous mushroom?"

I swallowed. "You know about aliens, right?"

Tony pulled out a stick of gum and unwrapped it. He offered me one. I shook my head.

He slid the gum onto his tongue and started chewing.

"Yeah," he said. "The skinny gray dudes. The ones you said freaked you out when you were little."

"Right," I said.

There was a moment of silence. Tony's gum smelled like strawberries. A bunch of teenagers came out of the bowling alley laughing and talking loudly, slapping each other's backs like they'd just scored a touchdown. I waited for them to pass.

"I think something happened," I continued. "We were camping, and I was getting some firewood. I saw a light, and then I remember, like, an owl was looking at me. It had these huge eyes. I couldn't make it go away. And then I passed out."

Tony's eyes widened. "Dude, are you serious?"

"When I woke up, there was this little hole in my stomach." I pulled up my shirt to show him. "I think they put an implant inside of me."

Tony leaned in, trying to get a closer look. "Can I touch it?"

"Better not," I said, and lowered my shirt.

He didn't say anything for a minute. He just sat there and chewed his gum. I thought he'd burst out laughing any second, but he didn't. "I believe you, hombre," he finally said.

He kept saying *hombre*, a word he picked up in Mexico, which meant "man."

I closed my eyes and let out a breath.

"You have to tell somebody," he said. "What about your

parents? I mean, they have to help you, right? Dude, you have to say something."

"I did. They thought I was crazy and took me to a doctor. They're making me take pills."

Tony bolted up. "Oh, man! That sucks! We gotta get you off of those. They're gonna turn your brains to mush!"

"I know."

And that's when I decided what to do.

CHAPTER SIXTEEN

WHILE I WAITED for the perfect opportunity to put my plan into effect, I had to suffer through taking the pills every day.

They were awful, and made me feel out of it.

I didn't know if it was a side effect or because I was thinking about aliens so much.

I just wanted it all to go away.

Days flew by. Summer would be over soon, and it'd be time to go back to school. The thought of it made me depressed.

About a week after talking to Tony, I finally got my chance.

Mom had one of her Ladies' Lunches, and after she left, I snuck into their bathroom.

And you know what I did?

I swapped out all the pills in the medicine bottles.

I replaced them with generic aspirin, vitamin C, and blue mints that were kind of oval-shaped. That was the hardest one to fake. I filled the bottles back up and flushed the real pills down the toilet. I watched them disappear in a little blue cyclone. When the water settled, one or two were still clinging to the side of the bowl, so I had to flush again. I knew Mom wouldn't notice the difference. She barely even looked at the pills when she gave them to me, and Dad never even saw them. He was hardly ever home anyway. He was always working.

I looked down at the swirling blue water. I knew what I was doing could get me in a whole bunch of trouble, but I didn't care. I suddenly felt in charge of myself for the first time in a while.

I have to say, it made me feel good.

It didn't take long to start feeling better. A few days later my headaches went away, and I didn't feel like I was moving through a big bowl of Jell-O. I felt normal again. Whatever that is. Then again, maybe it was all in my head anyway.

I dove back into my Max Hollyoak story. I just wanted to escape. You remember what happened last, don't you? My main character, Max, was playing with his dog in the park when they were chased by some kind of weird monster. It had floated right toward them, and no one else noticed it. And that's when something really strange happened. Max's dog, Alix, talked to him. She told him to follow her, and led him to safety.

III

The Message

Max slammed the front door and bounded up the stairs two at a time. Alix followed close behind, tracking wet paw prints all over the carpet.

"Mom!" Max cried.

No answer.

It's Sunday, he remembered. *She's at the grocery store.*

He closed his bedroom door and sat on the edge of the bed, then looked at Alix warily. "No," he said. "I know you didn't talk to me."

Alix cocked her head and stared up at him, her tongue lolling out of her mouth.

"Alix?"

No answer.

"Alix, did you talk to me?"

Max let out a long sigh and shook his head. He lay back on the bed and thought for a second that he should call his mom on her cell phone.

I hear you, Max

Max sat up, his heart in his chest.

I don't know why you can understand me now, the voice said. *I've tried talking to you before, but you never said anything back.*

Max closed his eyes. *I have to tell Mom. Something's wrong with me.*

He slid off the bed, crouched on one knee, and took Alix's wet head between his hands. "Alix, what's going on? How come I can hear you?"

There was a pause and then . . . *That thing. In the park. It is evil, Max. More evil than anything you could imagine. They are after you.*

"Who? Who's after me?"

Alix scratched behind her ear.

That's it, Max thought. *It's gone. I was imagining it.*

But then —

Mrs. Evans, from school. She can help. She is on your side.

Max flopped back onto the bed and buried his face in his pillow. "No! No! No!" he screamed. "This isn't real!"

For several long minutes, Max didn't move but just counted the heartbeats pounding in his ears. Finally, he turned over and stared up at the ceiling.

Was he going crazy?

First I'll talk to Mrs. Evans, he thought, and then shook his head in disbelief. *Alix said she's on my side.*

Whatever that means.

CHAPTER SEVENTEEN

I **WAS IN** the middle of playing *EverCraft* when a scream sent me reeling back from the computer.

Mom?

The Man in Black! He was in the house!

I rushed out of my room and bounded down the stairs without even thinking of the danger.

I stopped short in the living room, sliding across the hardwood floor in my socks.

Mom was hugging my brother, Edwin, home early from soccer camp in Germany.

She turned to me. "He's back!" she squealed.

I let out a long breath.

Edwin tried to wriggle out of her grasp. "Okay, okay," he said, "don't crush me, Mom."

He looked over at me. "Hey, kiddo."

. . .

Edwin told us that his original flight got canceled, and he had the chance to come home a few days early, so he decided to surprise us. He took a shuttle from the airport to the base so he wouldn't have to call Mom.

"How you doing, big guy?" he said, ruffling my hair. He had a smudge on his chin that I figured was his attempt at a little beard. It looked ridiculous.

"Okay," I said.

Mom looked at me closely when I said it, like she was checking to make sure I said the right thing. Edwin flopped down on the sofa. Mom took his suitcase and wheeled it out of the living room. I sat down beside him.

"Do you want something to drink, honey?" Mom called from the kitchen.

"Wine," Edwin called back. He looked at me and waggled his eyebrows. "Everybody in Europe drinks wine."

I didn't say anything. I suddenly remembered that I had absolutely nothing in common with my brother.

"Well, young man," Mom said a minute later, coming out of the kitchen, "you're not in Europe anymore. I'm afraid iced tea'll have to do."

She handed him a glass.

Edwin smirked and took a long sip.

"So," Mom said, sitting down on the couch between us and slapping her hands on her knees. "Tell us all about your trip. How was soccer camp?"

Edwin stroked his chin thoughtfully, then blew out a breath and told us about Germany. He was in a town called Freiburg, which he said was small but really pretty. "The Europeans only have coffee and a pastry in the morning," he said. "It's much more . . . sophisticated over there."

I did an internal eye roll.

He took another drink of iced tea, then placed the glass on the end table. "The soccer coach was really into films, so we saw a bunch of foreign movies at an old theater. You know, classic ones."

Mom's eyes lit up. "Really? So, what did you see? Fassbinder? Werner Herzog? What about *The Tin Drum*? That was one of my favorite films in college."

Edwin paused, at a loss for words. "Well, yeah," he said defensively. "We saw a lot of stuff."

I laughed inside. Edwin was trying to be all snooty, and Mom had set him straight. Mom looked at me and gave a private grin.

"What about you, buddy?" Edwin asked, punching me on the shoulder. "What've you been doing this summer?"

I rubbed my shoulder and then stared at my sneakers. "Uh, nothing. Just the usual stuff."

Mom bit her lip. I was sure she'd tell him everything later. *There are no secrets in this house,* Dad always said.

Edwin looked at me with fake amazement, his mouth hanging open. "You mean, you didn't run a marathon or join the local gym?"

"Ha-ha," I said. "Very funny."

Mom got up from the couch. "You must be starving. How's baked chicken and mashed potatoes sound?"

I could almost hear Edwin's stomach growl. "Awesome," he said.

A few days after Edwin got back, his new girlfriend came over for dinner. They'd started going out with each other right before he left for Germany. The only reason I knew she was his girlfriend was because I saw them down at the bowling alley smooching on each other.

Her name was Miranda, and she was pretty nice. She seemed completely different from Edwin, and I couldn't figure out what she liked about him. Maybe it was because he had that little fake beard and big muscles. Plus, he was on the soccer team. Girls liked guys who were into sports. At least it always seemed that way. Both Edwin and Dad thought that muscles were the only way to show that you were strong. You didn't need to have muscles to be strong. There were other ways. Ways they never thought about.

Mom cooked spaghetti and meatballs and put out the good plates. I was surprised she made meatballs because they were Dad's favorite and he wasn't there because he was working late.

Miranda handed Mom a platter with paper towels over it. "From my mother," she said.

"Smells de-lish," Mom said, taking the dish and peeking under the paper towel.

"It's keen-jeen," Miranda replied. I'd never heard the word before.

Mom cocked her head.

"It's a Brazilian dessert," Miranda explained, and then spelled it out for us. "*Q-u-i-n-d-i-m. Keen-jeen.*"

Edwin was all smiles. He looked like some kind of crazy lovebird or something.

"Sounds wonderful," Mom said, setting the platter on the kitchen counter. "So, is that where your family's from? Brazil?"

"Yes. My dad came here with his mother when he was a little boy. He got citizenship and then joined the Air Force."

I couldn't figure out Miranda before, because her skin was almost as dark as mine, but her hair was blond and straight. But now I got it. I knew Brazilians came in all kinds of shades because when I was into soccer, I used to watch the Brazilian national team on YouTube.

Mom's spaghetti was great, and I ate every noodle. I was in

a good mood for some reason. Maybe it was because I was off the meds I was supposed to be taking.

"So, what do you like to do?" Miranda asked me, about halfway through the dinner.

"Play video games all day," Edwin said under his breath.

"*Edwin*," Mom scolded him.

I stared at my plate.

"I like video games, too," Miranda said. "Do you play *Ever-Craft*?"

I almost dropped my fork. "You play *EverCraft*?"

Miranda thrust out her chin and sat up straighter. "You are talking to Arabella Thunderstorm, level-forty High Elf Paladin."

Mom and Edwin looked at each other and raised their eyebrows in unison.

After dinner, Miranda wanted to see my *EverCraft* character, so she came up to my room. I think it was the first time a girl had ever set foot in it. Except for Mom, who wasn't really a girl, anyway.

I loaded the game on my computer while Miranda checked out my room. It felt weird having her look at all my stuff. She was almost as tall as Edwin. She smelled nice, too, like lemons and strawberries. It must've been her shampoo or something. She picked up one of my books from the bedside table. "*The White Hart of Eldridge*," she said. "I read this. It's really good, right?"

"Yeah," I replied, surprised. So she liked computer games *and* fantasy books? Now I really didn't understand what she saw in Edwin. He thought reading books was a waste of time and that computer games were for nerds.

Miranda flipped through the pages. "Did you get to the part where—"

"Nope," I warned her, poking a finger in each ear. "No spoilers."

She laughed lightly and set the book down.

My character appeared on the screen in an animated swirl of blue and green smoke. "Here he is," I announced.

Miranda leaned over my shoulder. "Wow. He looks pretty badass. Druid, right?"

"Yeah. I like playing druids. Watch this."

For the next fifteen minutes, I showed Miranda all the cool stuff my character could do. I killed a couple goblins and even took down Rael the Ice Giant for the first time ever. I didn't tell her that, though. I acted like I did it all the time. She was really impressed, and I even let her play my character for a few minutes. Every now and then, she let out a small "*Oooh*" or "*Ahhh*," as she fought goblins and zombies.

It made me feel pretty good.

"Well," Miranda finally said, getting up from my desk, "I'd better get back downstairs. Thanks for showing me your room."

I smiled, but didn't reply. Miranda took one last look around and paused. "What's this?" she said, plucking a book from my shelf. It was the paperback of *Communion*, the one about the Grays — the one that got me started on all this alien business in the first place. "Do you believe all this stuff?"

I froze.

We were getting along fine, and now there was a chance I could ruin it. She'd think I was a freak. I mean, I knew she was Edwin's girlfriend and everything, but still, it would have been nice to have a new friend.

I opened my mouth, not sure what was going to come out. "I . . . I do," I stuttered.

Miranda cocked her head. There was a moment of silence. "I mean, are you *really* into it?"

I let out a little breath. *Here goes.* "Yes," I said. "There's a lot of stuff —"

"Ever heard of MUFON?" she interrupted.

I blinked.

"My dad's, like, head of the local chapter or something. He has people over once a month, and they talk about UFOs and aliens. Weird, huh?"

"Yeah," I said, stunned. "Weird."

CHAPTER EIGHTEEN

MUFON.

The Mutual UFO Network.

As soon as Miranda left, I looked them up. There were chapters all over the country. They researched and kept records of UFO sightings. I was surprised I hadn't heard of them.

Even if I wanted to talk to Miranda's dad, though, there was no way I could just go over there on my own. Maybe I could pretend like I wanted to cut their lawn and he'd answer the door or something. But then what would I say?

Hi, I'm Simon. I was abducted by aliens, and they put an implant inside of me. Nice to meet you.

No freakin' way.

Maybe I could just come right out and *ask* Miranda. Tell her that I wanted to see her character in *EverCraft* and then somehow sit in on one of her dad's meetings. That'd be weird, though, right? I'm just a twelve-year-old kid. What would they think?

I got the chance when I least expected it.

It happened when Miranda came over a few nights later. She looked pretty. Her lipstick was shiny, and her hair had that nice smell again, like strawberries. She and Edwin were going to a movie. Edwin was getting ready in the bathroom, which left me and Miranda alone.

"Simon," Miranda whispered. We were sitting at the kitchen table. Mom and Dad were out at some military reception or something. Mom called it an awards banquet.

"Yeah?" I ventured.

"Remember I was telling you about my dad?"

I nodded.

"Well, I told him about you."

"You what?"

"I told him that Edwin's brother was into UFOs and that maybe you'd want to come to a meeting."

My ears suddenly got hot. I heard the squeak of the faucet in the bathroom turning on and then running water. Miranda glanced toward the door. "And what'd he say?" I asked.

"He said, 'No problem.'"

She smiled, showing perfect teeth. "You have to stay for

dinner, though. Anyone who comes into the house has to eat, according to my mom."

Edwin appeared in a cloud of sweet, overbearing cologne. I thought I was going to puke. Miranda wrinkled her nose.

"*Really?*" Edwin said when Miranda told him I'd be coming over.

"I just want to show him some of my fantasy books," Miranda said innocently. She flipped her hair and gave a shy smile. Edwin immediately got all dreamy-eyed.

Amazing.

Girls could get guys to do stuff just by flipping their hair.

A few days later, I went over to Miranda's house with Edwin. He drove and tried to act like Dad by putting on loud rock music. He even leaned his elbow out of the car just like Dad. We barely said anything to each other on the way over. I thought that was pretty pitiful. My only brother, and we didn't have anything to talk about.

Miranda's mom and dad were older than mine, but they seemed a lot cooler. Her mom had a green stripe through her hair, which was really weird for someone who lived on an Air Force base. Her dad was on disability from work. I didn't know what his problem was, but he had a brace on his back and moved like he was walking on eggshells. His shirt said

ROLLING STONES in red letters with a tongue sticking out. A small hoop earring pierced his left ear. They also burned these sticks of what Miranda called incense. It smelled like burnt wood. I thought it'd trigger my asthma, but it was okay.

I looked around their living room. There was a pile of ancient computer monitors in one corner with a bunch of tangled cords. Some old sewing machines sat in another area. Wooden crates with fruit labels held tons of magazines, and some artwork that looked like it was painted by a four-year-old hung on the wall. It was supposed to be a fish. I think. "Folk art," Miranda called it. A bunch of leafy plants were on the windowsills, and a few sat in planters on chairs with the stuffing coming out. But even though it was a mess, it didn't seem dirty. Just cluttered. Mom would freak out if she saw this place. I wondered what the base inspectors said when they came by to check things out.

Dinner was Brazilian tacos stuffed with olives, green onions, peppers, and sour cream. I didn't think I'd ever eat anything called sour cream, but I did. The funny thing? It wasn't even sour. That just doesn't make sense. *Why do they call it sour cream if it isn't sour?*

Edwin tried to impress Miranda's parents by talking about art he'd seen in Germany. Her dad nodded along and mentioned a place in Brazil called Serra da Capivara, where you could see prehistoric paintings. That made me think of a documentary I saw all about cave paintings in France. It was called *The Cave of Forgotten Dreams*, and the people who made the movie were the first ones to ever go inside and film it. It was amazing. Just looking at the paintings, I could imagine what it must have been like to live back then. The thing I found strange was that all the art only showed animals like horses and giant woolly mammoths, but never any people. Why didn't the artists ever draw themselves? I always wondered about that.

I didn't say a whole lot while we ate, even though Miranda's mom asked me a bunch of questions. "I mostly just like to read," I said. She looked at me and smiled. She had dark brown skin and pretty eyes. A green stone hung from a chain around her neck. "Well, no wonder you and Miranda get along," she said. "Miranda was reading before she could walk."

Miranda smiled and looked a little embarrassed.

After dinner, Miranda's dad went down into the basement, and she pulled me aside while Edwin helped her mom clear the table. "You ready?" she asked.

"I guess so," I said. "What's Edwin gonna think?"

"I told him Dad has a sci-fi book club."

I stared at my sneakers, uncertain about all of this.

"Look," Miranda said, "don't worry. If you want to leave, I'll be upstairs. Just tell him you have to go. No problem, right?"

"Right," I said, trying to sound confident. "No problem."

The basement was small, with dark wood paneling, just like ours. All the houses on the base looked the same, unless you were an officer or somebody with a high rank. A shabby brown couch and a few mismatched chairs were spread around a folding metal table. There were books everywhere — stacked on the floor and bulging from the dark shelves against one wall. There was also a poster of that old show called *The X-Files* that said I WANT TO BELIEVE, and another one with three gray aliens looking out of a spaceship window. A mounted deer head on the wall looked at me with big sad eyes.

I took a deep breath and glanced around at the people who were gathered down there already. One woman reminded me of my Grannie Claire. She had a ball of yarn in her lap and was knitting what seemed to be a big sweater. She gave me a warm smile. A blond guy, probably about Edwin's age, sat in an office chair with wheels on it. He was as thin as a snake, and wore a tank-top, which showed pale green tattoos running up and down his white arms. Dad's military friends were the only people I ever saw with tattoos. Dad had one on his left shoulder. It was the head of an eagle with some numbers under it. "To commemorate my brothers," he'd said when I asked him about it once.

The blond guy looked like the kind of person you'd want to

stay away from. He seemed jumpy. One of his legs was bouncing up and down like a jackhammer.

A side door that led out into the backyard opened with a squeak, and two more people came in.

"Hey, Jerry," Miranda's dad called out. "How you doing, Margie?"

Jerry and Margie took seats on the couch. They both smiled at me. Jerry wore a green flight suit. *Was he a pilot?* Margie — his wife, I supposed — was taller than he was, with long brown hair hanging all the way down her back.

I suddenly wondered if anyone here was on meds, like I was supposed to be.

What would Dad say if he found out I was down here with a bunch of people I didn't know?

But I was with Edwin, I told myself. He was right upstairs.

Once everybody was seated, Miranda's dad took off his back brace and flopped into a saggy cushioned chair. He let out a big breath. "Everyone, this is Simon, Miranda's friend. Simon, everyone."

They all smiled, except for the nervy blond guy, whose leg was still tapping away, like he was trying to dig a hole through the carpet. I swallowed and tried to force a smile.

"Miranda said you were interested in aliens?" her father asked me. "Well, you've come to the right place." He waved his hand like a game show model. "These are all believers, Simon."

My palms were sweating. He just came right out and said it like he was asking me if I liked baseball or something. *But these people were like me, right?* Not like Mom and Dad, who didn't believe me. My insides felt all jittery.

"So, have you had any experiences?" the man in the flight suit, Jerry, asked. "Any encounters?"

I fiddled with my hands. *Maybe I should get up and go. Miranda said she'd be right upstairs.* "We were camping," I started. "Me and my mom and dad. They told me to go get some firewood."

Nervy Guy's eyes suddenly got a little wider. Yarn Lady nodded her head a little, like she was encouraging me. "It's okay, honey," she said. "You can trust us. We're all believers, like Ricky said."

Ricky. Miranda's dad. I heard his wife call him that upstairs.

I wrung my hands together. "Well, so, I was walking in the woods, and I saw a light. I knew it wasn't the moon because it was too bright."

Miranda's dad moved in his chair and let out a little grunt, like his back was hurting. "Ah-ha." He winced.

"And then I saw an owl," I said.

"The eyes." Nervy Guy finally spoke. "Always the eyes."

"Burke's right," Miranda's dad added. "Abductees often see all kinds of animals. Owls. Cats. They're false memories, put there by the aliens."

Burke. Nervy Guy didn't seem like a Burke. Then again, I'd never even met a Burke before.

"One experiencer said she saw Mr. Peanut," announced Margie, the woman who'd come in with Jerry. "That was a false memory, too."

"Mr. Peanut?" I asked.

"The Mr. Peanut character wears a monocle and has a face that resembles an alien," explained Burke, looking warily around the room, like aliens were about to come out of the walls and carry him away.

I paused. *Maybe these people were crazy.* The thought of Mr. Peanut coming into my room in the middle of the night terrified me.

"What else do you remember?" Miranda's dad asked.

"I heard a voice inside my head. It said to remain calm. That's all I remember before I blacked out. When I woke up, I had a scoop mark on my stomach."

Yarn Lady stopped knitting.

"I think they put an implant inside of me," I finished, my mouth suddenly dry.

Silence filled the room. I heard the footsteps of someone walking around upstairs.

"A few days later, I saw a Man in Black."

"An MIB." Miranda's dad shook his head, as if troubled.

"They're not human. They're a hybrid species working with our government."

My head spun.

This was real. I was actually talking to people who believed in aliens. I wasn't alone anymore.

"The implant," Margie asked. "Were you able to get it out?"

"We know a scientist on the base," Jerry added. "He could study it."

This was all happening too fast. Just twenty minutes ago, I thought no one could ever understand what I was going through, and now —

"No," I started. "I haven't . . . I haven't tried to do that. I —"

"Okay, everyone," Miranda's dad said, holding up a hand. "Let's not move too fast. Simon's new to all this. We don't want to overwhelm him."

I had to admit, I was glad he said that, and it made me breathe a little easier. I stared at all of them for a minute. Burke was still bouncing his leg, eyes flitting every which way.

"What do they want?" I asked.

Everyone in the room stared at me.

"The aliens," I continued. "What do they want with us?"

"Simon," Miranda's dad said, "we believe an incredible moment in human history is coming. They are making themselves known. It's only a matter of time before Planet X is revealed for the threat it really is."

"Planet X?"

"Nibiru," said Burke. "Nibiru is the home planet of the Grays."

Nibiru, I thought. *Why is that familiar?*

"It's a giant planet just beyond our solar system," Miranda's dad said, "and has a mass twenty times greater than Earth. It has an orbit of three thousand, six hundred years. Soon it will enter our system. When that happens, Earth will suffer catastrophic environmental collapse." He paused. The room was deathly silent, but for Burke's nervous tapping. "Then they will begin."

I swallowed. "Begin what?"

More silence.

"To claim this planet," Miranda's dad finally said. "And to turn what's left of the human race into slaves."

CHAPTER NINETEEN

PEOPLE KEPT TALKING but I didn't really hear what they were saying. I sat motionless, stunned. *Did they really believe the aliens were coming to conquer us?*

Nibiru. I'd heard it somewhere before, but I couldn't remember where. It was an itch in my brain I couldn't scratch.

The thump of shoes clomping on stairs snapped me out of the moment.

I turned toward the sound. Miranda stood at the bottom of the steps. Her eyes landed on me. "Edwin's ready to go," she said. "Simon, are you ready?"

Miranda's father shifted in his seat again. "Oh," he said, looking at me. "Already? We've got a lot more to discuss. Lots of stuff you need to know, Simon."

I looked quickly to Miranda and then back to her dad. "Yeah," I said. "I should leave when my brother does."

The group of UFO believers all smiled and nodded.

I blushed, but I'm not sure anyone saw it, because of my skin color.

"Ready, Simon?" Miranda asked.

"Yeah," I said, getting up. My legs felt like rubber.

"Great to meet you, Simon," Jerry said.

"Let us know if you remember anything else," Miranda's dad added.

I gave a quick nod to the others and followed Miranda up the stairs.

Back home, I wondered if those MUFON members were nuts. They thought aliens were coming to turn us into slaves after their planet enters our solar system. *When that happens, Earth will suffer catastrophic environmental collapse.*

If that were true, wouldn't scientists be freaking out about it?

But then I remembered Roswell. They didn't want us to know. They just wanted to keep us blind and in the dark.

I met up with Tony at the bowling alley that weekend. He wanted to know everything that was going on.

Did the aliens come yet?

Did you feel it when they put the implant inside of you?

What are you going to do next?

I didn't have answers for any of his questions.

We were sitting with our backs up against the brick wall near the bicycle racks. Tony cracked his knuckles, like a cartoon character preparing for a fight. "I got an idea, hombre."

"What?"

"You know where you went camping? At Cape Henlopen?"

"Yeah."

"We have to go back there. We might find some kind of evidence the aliens left behind."

I froze. That was the last thing I wanted to do.

But . . .

He was right. I hadn't even thought about going back, because I was too scared.

"Maybe they left footprints or something," Tony continued.

"I don't think aliens leave footprints."

"Well, maybe they left *something*. Like, some kind of alien tech. We won't know unless we check it out, right?"

He had a point. Even the smallest clue could be huge.

"Right," I finally said.

And I knew just who could help us.

CHAPTER TWENTY

WHEN I ASKED Miranda about going to Cape Henlopen with me and Tony, she was up for it.

"I'll tell your mom and dad that I can keep an eye on you guys," she said. "I'm seventeen now. I have a driver's license."

I didn't think I needed anyone to "keep an eye" on me. She had a car, and that was the important thing.

But there was something else I had to do first.

See Dr. Cross again.

I was supposed to go twice a month, and my next appointment was a day before our mission. I was a little afraid that she'd know I wasn't on the pills. *Could she tell? Did doctors have some kind of skill where they could see if you were taking your meds?*

I was nervous the night before the visit. She'd try to talk to me again. Maybe she'd want to give me more drugs. I shook my head. If she knew the things the MUFON members talked about, she'd try to have them all put in an insane asylum.

Before Mom took me to see Dr. Cross, she made breakfast. Bacon and eggs. "C'mon," she said, putting a plate in front of me. "Let's eat first. Get the day started right."

Dad had already left for work. My stomach rumbled. I was surprised I was hungry, because I hadn't been eating that much lately. Sunshine came in through the little kitchen window and fell on the table in slanted rays. I dug into the food. Mom studied me over her coffee cup. "So, you've been feeling okay?" she asked.

"Uh-huh," I grunted around a slice of bacon. She sipped her coffee. "Do you feel like the pills are helping?"

"Sure," I said. "I'm better now."

I felt bad for not telling Mom the truth. She was doing everything she could to help me and I was totally betraying her with my lies.

Mom smiled and reached out to place her hand over mine.

I continued to eat, but no matter how much I shoveled in my mouth, I felt like something inside of me couldn't be filled up.

Back in the cold white room, I was reminded of how awful it was the first time I was here.

"Hello, Simon," Dr. Cross greeted me. "Have a seat."

I sat down in a fancy black metal chair. I put my hands together.

The uncomfortable silence fell over us again, just like the first time. Dr. Cross tried to get me talking. For the next forty-five minutes, she peppered me with questions, all the while balancing her little notepad on her crossed knees.

How was I eating?

Did I have any questions about my medication?

Was I sleeping more or less than before I first came in?

She never once said anything about *aliens*.

I replied with one-word answers.

Finally, my time was up.

"We'll see you next time, Simon," Dr. Cross said, defeated. "I hope that maybe you can share a little more on your next visit. Okay?"

"Okay," I said, knowing I'd do nothing of the sort.

CHAPTER TWENTY-ONE

BEFORE TONY, MIRANDA, and I set out, I needed to come up with a destination — someplace to tell Mom we were going. Cape Henlopen was about an hour away, so we'd be gone for a while. I couldn't say we were going back there. She'd think that was suspicious. So I got on the Internet and looked at a map. There were several possibilities for an innocent summer day trip. Assateague Island was the best choice. I'd been there before with my parents and Edwin, and it was pretty cool. There were a bunch of wild horses that people said were descendants of horses that were on a Spanish ship that wrecked a long time ago. No one knew for sure, though. When I saw them, I imagined chasing one down in my bare feet, and then swinging myself onto its back and riding off to find an adventure. I'd probably fall off though, since I'm not very athletic.

Edwin rolled his eyes when he learned Miranda was taking

us, but she told him that it was fun to hang out with some-one who shared her love of fantasy and sci-fi books. Plus, she reminded him, he said he was going to hang out with some of his soccer friends, anyway.

He just looked at her and got that dazed expression again. God, he was a pushover.

Mom was hesitant at first. "Make sure Miranda obeys the speed limit, okay? And call me if you're going to be late coming home or if you get stuck in traffic."

Even though she was a little nervous about us going, she thought it was great that Edwin's girlfriend showed such an interest in me. The day before our trip, I overheard her talking to Dad in the living room when I came out of the bathroom. "It's nice," Mom was saying. "Simon's shy and sensitive. A girl like Miranda can help him in social situations. You know. In the future, with girls his own age."

I couldn't see them, but I imagined Dad smirking at that. Plus, I didn't really think about girls anyway.

Mom packed lunches and gave us a cooler full of sodas and water. "It's good you're doing something with friends," she said. "I knew Dr. Cross would be able to help."

And then she hugged me.

I felt bad. I was lying. And I wasn't taking my medicine. Every time I saw Dad—which wasn't a lot because he was really busy at work lately—all he ever said was "Are you taking your pills?" When I told him I was, he said, "Good. You'll be right as rain in no time." That was it for our conversations. He never said anything else about my "incident."

He just didn't seem to care one way or the other.

Before we left, when Mom went down to the basement to grab a cooler, Miranda turned to me. "Look," she said. "I know something happened to you, or else you wouldn't be interested in meeting my dad's group. But you don't have to tell me what happened if you don't want to."

I nibbled my lip. She was one of the few people I could talk to about aliens. She deserved to know. "I think aliens put an implant inside of me," I told her. "When I was on a camping trip with my parents."

It felt like a great weight had just come off my chest. Miranda didn't seem surprised, or look at me like I was crazy.

"What else do you remember?"

"Just a voice, telling me to stay calm and not to move. It sounded like it came from inside my head. I saw an owl, too."

There was a moment of silence. "*Owls*," Miranda whispered. "Dad says aliens implant false memories in people so they think they had some kind of encounter with an animal to cover up their abductions."

"So you believe in aliens, too?"

Miranda let out a sympathetic sigh. "I don't know if I believe in aliens, but I believe in you, Simon."

I have to say, that made me feel pretty good.

I checked my wallet to make sure I had my ID card before we left. I'd need it to get back on the base. Dad says a military ID is the best form of identification to have, and that you can get out of a lot of trouble by having one with you at all times. I still remember when I got mine. The picture on it doesn't look like me anymore. My cheeks were chubbier back then. I was actually smiling, which seems weird. *Why was I smiling?* I think I was excited to get an ID. It's like what they call "a rite of passage" in books.

Miranda pulled up to the main gate, and a guy in a blue military uniform came out of his little booth and took our IDs. We were *leaving* the base, so technically, he didn't need to look at our identification. I guess since we were kids he thought he could do whatever he wanted. His scalp was red, and his hair was in a buzz cut — high and tight, they called it. Just like Dad's. He'd tried to make me get a cut like that once, but Mom came to my rescue.

The guard looked at each card for what seemed like forever. *Jeez.* It was like in the movies. Every now and then, he'd look up from the ID and study our faces, like he had to make sure it was a match. *Did he think we were terrorists or something?* I guessed it would be pretty boring standing in that booth all day long, and I doubted he was allowed to sit down and read comic books or anything. Finally, he gave us back our cards. "You kids be careful out there," he said, looking over the tops of his aviator sunglasses.

"We will," Miranda said with a smile.

Miranda drove an old yellow Volkswagen. "A Beetle," she called it, and said it belonged to her parents in the '80s and still ran like new. She drove real slow, with both hands on the wheel. Maybe she thought it'd fly away, like that car in the Harry Potter books, if she let go.

We were on the main highway, which was called Route 13. We passed fast food restaurants, shopping malls, auto parts stores, car washes, tobacco outlets, and gun shops. It seemed crazy to me that you could just walk in there and buy a gun, but Dad said that was the great thing about America: "the right to bear arms."

The sun was blazing hot, and I felt it on my neck and shoulders as I sat in the front. Tony was stretched out in the middle of the back seat, arms spread out to either side. "So you're Edwin's girlfriend?" he asked Miranda.

"I guess you could say that," she answered.

"Hmpf," Tony muttered. "And you're into *EverCraft*?"

"Yup," Miranda answered. "Level-forty High Elf Paladin."

"Wow," Tony said, impressed. "Did you do all of the raids in the Caves of Ashmorg?"

"Uh-huh."

"What about the pariahs on Widow's Peak?"

"Wasn't a problem."

Tony paused. I had to admit, this talk was even a little too geeky for me.

"Sounds like you know your stuff," he said. "We should all do a raid together some night."

"I wish I could," Miranda replied. "I'm in a guild, though, and I promised to only do raids with my group members."

"Well, maybe you could create an alt. You know, another character."

Miranda nodded to herself. "Yeah. Maybe."

The rhythm of the road made me doze off for a minute, but I woke up when we slowed down. The exits on the highway had thinned out to campgrounds and nature preserves. One of them was for a wildlife refuge called Prime Hook that Mom and Dad took me to when we first moved here. Mom said it was the largest tidal salt marsh in the Mid-Atlantic. I saw a bald eagle there once, and for weeks afterward, that's all I would talk about. It was incredible, and I couldn't get over how big its wingspan was.

We didn't talk much, and as slow as Miranda was driving, I thought we'd never get there. I fiddled with my phone for a while, but got bored pretty quickly and then just stared out the window. I guess I could have asked Miranda what her favorite fantasy books were, but I didn't. I got self-conscious all of a sudden for some reason. The nice smell of her hair made me nervous. Plus she was pretty.

The landmarks became more familiar. I thought back to driving here with Mom and Dad. I never wanted to go. But they made me. And I had an alien encounter.

Right before we took the exit, I saw a dead deer on the side of the road. It made me sad. It also made me think of the Grays and their weird abductions of cows and farm animals. *Why do they do that?*

"We must be close," Tony said, interrupting my thoughts.

After another few minutes on a dirt road, Miranda pulled the car into a parking lot. Sand and gravel crunched under the tires. I recognized the little office that Dad had gone into when we were here. He'd come back out with a safety folder, I remembered. Miranda maneuvered the car between two big trucks and shut off the engine. She blew out a breath.

"Ready?" she asked.

The sun was still high as we headed into the woods. I was glad it wasn't dark. I really didn't think I could go there at night again.

A few families with little kids were setting up tents and starting campfires. Music drifted through the air, country songs mostly, which I kind of liked. We found the campsite from a few weeks ago and then took the little path I'd used to get the firewood. Tony's eyes darted around the forest. "Where was it, hombre? Where'd they grab you?"

My stomach fluttered. "I don't remember being grabbed. I just remember waking up."

I led the way, with Miranda behind me and Tony bringing up the rear. The sun blazed on my neck, and little gnats buzzed around my head. I scanned the ground as we walked. A sense of unease settled over me, like a spider's web. I stopped on the path. We were there. I remembered it clearly.

"Here?" Miranda ventured.

"I think so," I said. I dug the toe of my sneaker in the dirt, looking for who-knew-what.

I remembered the voice I'd heard that night. *QUIET. REMAIN STILL.*

It was a cold, flat voice — one that came from inside my head, but didn't sound like me.

We stood in a circle. The sun cast shadows of tree branches on the forest floor.

"What are we looking for?" Tony asked.

"I don't know," I said. "It was your idea to come here."

I looked up into the heights of the towering trees — the

trees where I'd seen an owl. *But was it really an owl, or a gray alien with black eyes and a slit for a mouth?*

"Quiet!" Miranda suddenly hissed. "Hide!"

She grabbed my shirt and pulled me off the path, behind a cluster of bushes and small trees. Tony darted after us.

"Get down," she whispered.

We all dropped to the ground. A sharp branch poked me in the chest. "What the —" Tony said in a hushed tone. "Why are you —"

Three men with uniforms and walkie-talkies appeared on the trail. They were scanning the ground, like they were looking for something. Keys jangled on their belts, and their steps were heavy, breaking twigs and branches as they passed us. Their uniforms were black, without any kind of badges or symbols. *Who were they? Had they seen us?*

I felt a trickle of sweat down my back. Tony's breathing was so loud I was just waiting for us to get caught. I didn't even want to nudge him because that would probably make him jump. Miranda knelt on one knee and was absolutely still and silent, like some kind of statue.

I peered through the bushes. One of the men was holding some kind of small box and pointing it at the ground as he walked. I knew what it was. A radiation detector. I saw them in movies all the time.

"Reading's clear here," one man said.

"Let's get back," said another. "Don't see why they sent us in the first place."

One of them lit a cigarette, and the sharp smell burned my nostrils. *People shouldn't smoke in the woods,* I thought to myself.

"Who called this in?" the one with the radiation detector asked.

"Jaworski," the smoker replied. "Over at ATIC."

"Jaworski," the man sneered. "Always Jaworski on this kind of stuff."

"Mirage conditions again," said the other guy, and all three of them laughed. "Swamp gas."

A heavy sigh, and then, "I think it's beer o'clock, fellas."

"Amen."

I heard their crunching footsteps as they walked away, talking among themselves. We stayed silent. Frozen. Barely breathing. It was deathly quiet. I didn't even hear any birds. Finally, when at least three minutes had passed, I got up.

"Coast is clear," I whispered.

We all crept to the spot where they'd been standing. I brushed leaves and dirt from my pants. I looked at the ground and then up above at the twisting tree branches.

"This is it," I said.

"What?" Tony and Miranda asked at the same time.

"This is the exact spot where I passed out."

"I thought you said it was over there," Miranda huffed, pointing. "Where we were just standing."

"No," I said, staring at the ground. "It was here. I know it."

A burst of static exploded from a walkie-talkie.

"Hey, you kids!" a man's voice boomed through the trees.

"Run!" Tony shouted.

We took off, back the way we came. I'd never run so fast in my life. Tree branches whipped out at my face. Tony was in the front, kicking up dirt and pebbles. Miranda was behind him, and I was last, arms and legs pumping furiously. Up ahead, the Beetle sat like a big yellow lemon in the parking lot.

"Hurry, hombres!" Tony called.

He flung open the passenger door and scurried in, then reached across and unlocked the driver's side for Miranda. I scrambled into the back seat and closed the door. The men in uniforms burst out of the woods like a group of Orcs in *The Lord of the Rings*.

"Go! Go! Go!" Tony shouted.

Miranda revved the engine and pulled out, leaving a cloud of dirt and dust behind us.

I fished in my pocket for my inhaler and gave myself

a blast. I breathed in as the mist hit the back of my throat. *One . . . two . . . three . . . exhale.*

"You all right, hombre?" Tony asked, turning around.

I breathed in and out again and then relaxed my shoulders. "Yeah," I panted. "Just gotta catch my breath."

I laid my head back. My arms were scraped from the jagged edges of tree branches. Miranda was breathing hard, her shoulders rising and falling. Sweat slicked the back of her neck. I gave myself another blast of the inhaler, even though I was supposed to wait a few minutes between doses.

"Those were military guys!" Tony exclaimed.

"But why were they there?" I asked. "Why were they off-base? What's ATIC?"

"Oh, man," Tony said, rocking back and forth. "This is bad."

"Don't worry," Miranda said. "They didn't see our faces."

"Maybe they saw your license plate," I said.

Miranda didn't say anything. But by the way she gripped the wheel, I could tell she was freaked out.

We were silent on the way home. We hadn't been gone that long. I'd have to explain to Mom why we were back so early, unless we just drove around for a long time. But as the roads became more familiar, it didn't seem like Miranda was going to do that. She just looked straight ahead and didn't say anything.

She dropped off Tony first, who told me to stay safe and to "fight the power," as he got out of the car. It was just another block to my house, and when we arrived, Miranda and I sat in the driveway for a minute.

"Something's going on," she said. "I don't know what, but I'm going to tell my dad about it. Maybe he'll have some answers."

"Who do you think they were?" I asked. I was worried.

"I don't know," she replied, staring through the windshield.

I nodded but didn't say anything. I felt numb. "Thanks," I said. "Thanks for taking us . . . and believing me."

She reached out and actually rubbed my head, like I was her pet dog or something. "No problem, kiddo," she said. She must've gotten that from Edwin.

I got out and closed the door. It sounded incredibly loud for some reason. I turned to wave when I got to the doorstep, but Miranda had already pulled away.

I opened the front door. Mom and Dad were sitting at the kitchen table. I gulped.

Pill bottles.

All three of them.

Lined up in a little row.

"You want to explain this, champ?" Dad said.

CHAPTER TWENTY-TWO

I **STOOD** at the table. Frozen.

"You want to sit down, Simon?" Mom asked.

She was disappointed. I could tell by the little frown lines around her face. I pulled out a chair. It scraped across the floor, echoing in the room.

Dad took a swig from his beer and then set it down. He just stared at me, waiting.

"I was sick of taking them," I said. "They made me feel like —like I wasn't really myself."

"This is majorly FUBAR, son," Dad said.

I didn't know what that meant. It must've been another one of his military terms, like Bravo Zulu, which meant "Great job." He never said that to me, though, only to Edwin. Another one was FTA: "failure to adapt," which he used for me all the time.

"I thought we were making progress," Mom said. Her

voice broke. She rested both elbows on the table and cradled her chin in her hands. And then she started crying.

I'd done it now.

"I'm sorry, Mom," I said softly.

She shook her head back and forth and wiped away a tear with the back of her hand. Dad looked at me like I was the biggest loser in the world. "Go up to your room, Simon," he said quietly, like he was exhausted. "Do you think you can do that without messing up?"

I studied the swirls in the kitchen table. Mom was still sniffling. Her shoulders were trembling. She looked up, and her eyes were red.

"Upstairs!" Dad shouted, and a vein throbbed on his forehead. "Now!" This just made Mom cry more.

The chair scraped back and I headed upstairs, my legs as heavy as lead.

I sat up in bed, my back propped against the headboard. What did I have to do to convince them I wasn't crazy?

I just saw military guys in the woods where I was taken! It was real!

I'd be grounded, that was for sure. The only other time I'd been grounded was when Tony and I went looking for giant horseshoe crab shells at a place called Port Mahon. We went with his older brother, Calvin, and had to leave the base to get there. I hadn't told Mom and Dad I was going, and when I got back, they were furious. Well, Dad was. Mom just looked disappointed. That hurt worse, you know? Screaming and yelling is one thing, but when your mom gives you that look that only moms can give, well, you know you've messed up.

It didn't matter if I got grounded. I never went anywhere, anyway.

I felt an itch under my shirt where a branch must have jabbed me. I raised my shirt to scratch it, but my hand drifted to the little hole instead. It was still there. I touched it.

NIBIRU, I heard inside my head.

Images flashed in front of my eyes.

And then I remembered.

The owl in my room . . .

White mist . . .

Lying on a cold metal slab . . .

It all came flashing back.

The aliens studying me, poking me.

They opened my mouth and looked inside.

I had been abducted again!

I'd wet the bed that night.

And I only now just remembered.

I ONLY NOW JUST REMEMBERED!

My insides were churning like a swarm of bees.

It all came back to me. The inside of the ship, the white curving walls, the whir of machines. "No," I whispered.

I looked at my arm. A gray alien had scraped my skin there. I ran my fingers across it. It looked red, like I had fallen down and hurt myself.

A scent came up in my nose, like wet mushrooms. That was their smell.

Oh God. They'd come back for me, and I hadn't even known it!

I had to get it out of me . . .

The implant.

They were tracking me . . .

They could come back anytime they wanted to.

And now there were secret military people in the woods?

It was real.

IT WAS ALL REAL!

I sprinted from the bed to my desk.

I pulled open the top drawer and rooted through the old action figures, yo-yos, rubber bands, paper clips, old candy wrappers, and little toy cars.

There.

Scissors.

Open, like a V.

I picked them up.

Lifted my shirt.

I exhaled, and pressed the point of the blade against my stomach.

First, a little knick, then deeper.

It didn't really hurt.

I closed my eyes.

Pressed deeper.

The blade went in.

I looked down.

RED.

Everything was red.

Red was all I could see.

PART THREE

CHAPTER TWENTY-THREE

BEEP

BEEP

BEEP

Beep . . . beep . . . beep . . .

I was in a bed, but not my bed.

This was not my room.

Machines.

Bright light.

A window.

. . . beep . . . beep . . .

Sharp pain in my stomach.

A burning.

Like a flame, too close to my skin.

The odor of alcohol mixed with soap hung in the air like poison.

"Simon."

"*Simon.*"

The voice was close . . . but faint.

"Simon?"

Mom's face came into focus. She took my hand. I was in a hospital bed. There were tubes and wires all around me. A needle was in my arm, held in place by a bandage. A dot of red bloomed from it.

Blood.

I turned my head to the right. A clear bag of liquid hung from a pole. I was hooked up to an IV.

"Mom?" I said.

"Shhh," she whispered. "You need to rest, Simon."

She touched my forehead, which was damp with sweat. I tried to move and felt the sharp pain in my stomach again.

"Careful," Mom said. "You've got stitches."

And then I remembered.

My room . . .

Scissors . . .

Red.

Everything went red.

"Did you find it?" I croaked out.

Mom leaned in. "Find what?"

"The implant. Did I get it out?"

Mom drew away and released a trembling breath. She closed and then opened her eyes slowly. She looked like she hadn't slept in days. "Sleep now, Simon," she whispered. "Everything's going to be all right."

And that's what I did.

Slept.

I had dreams of being on the alien ship — the white walls, the whirring sound.

Whir . . . whir . . . click.

They had me strapped down to a bed or something. I remembered feeling helpless. Scared. They had studied me like a lab rat.

NIBIRU.

The same word Miranda's dad had said. A great calamity was coming.

I drifted in and out of consciousness. I was thinking about my story, *Max Hollyoak and the Tree of Everwyn.* I was imagining the next chapter. *Did I dream that, or have I already written that part?*

I wasn't sure. Everything seemed all mixed up.

A man came into my room and gave me some ice chips. He was in a white uniform. Dr. Cross, the psychiatrist lady, came by and tried to talk to me, but I didn't say anything. I didn't want to talk to her. Then again, maybe I imagined her being there. Maybe everything was a dream and I was living inside of it, trapped.

They kept me in the hospital for two days. They said I needed a quiet place to recover.

They thought I had tried to kill myself.

That wasn't true. I was just trying to get the implant out.

I wasn't crazy. There were military people in the woods, for God's sake. What was ATIC? *Mirage conditions,* one of them had said. *Swamp gas.*

They were there to check out UFO activity.

They knew.

They all knew, and they were hiding it from the public.

CHAPTER TWENTY-FOUR

BACK HOME, I was confined to my room. I had six stitches. Every time I told Mom that I'd never try to do something as crazy as kill myself, she just shushed me, like a baby. "It's going to be all right," she said. "You're going to see Dr. Cross again soon. She can help, Simon."

That just made me feel worse.

I looked all around the room as soon as I got back, and didn't see anything strange or suspicious. But you know what? I read somewhere that sometimes these implants just kind of dissolve once they're taken out of your body. They're made from alien tech we don't even understand.

Edwin came into my room and sat down and tried to talk to me, but it was all a bunch of sports nonsense, like "Keep your head up, champ," and, "You'll be back in the game soon."

I didn't care about his dumb sports crap. I just wanted to sleep.

Tony texted me the next day:

> hombre what happened? u ok?

> how did u know?

> edwin told miranda and she told me.

> i tried to cut out the implant.

> dude!

> i remembered something. campground wasn't only time i was abducted. happened few weeks ago too. it was blocked out.

> dude im comin over

> mom wont let anyone see me. said i have to rest.

Even after I started feeling better, Mom wouldn't let me do anything. She waited on me hand and foot. I felt bad. I didn't want her to do that, but she did it anyway.

Something else happened, too.

They put me back on the meds.

This time, I took them. I had to. Mom kept a close eye on the pills. I didn't even know where she was keeping them. But she watched me swallow them every single time.

I didn't know what to do with myself. I stayed in my room mostly, but one time I went out in the backyard and sat on the deck. I looked up at the sky and tried to lose myself in the clouds. I did that a lot when I was little. I'd stare for as long as I could without blinking until a cloud turned into a shape. It was almost like I could control what the shape would become — a boat, a car, a knight on horseback. I stared and stared for several minutes, but no matter how hard I tried, the clouds didn't change.

After a few more days, Mom finally allowed Tony to come visit. It felt like it'd been forever since we'd seen each other.

"Hombre," he said, sitting down at my desk. "You okay, man?"

"Yeah," I said, sitting up. I winced.

Tony looked at me with wide eyes. "Did you get it out? The implant?"

It felt weird hearing him say that. I talked about it inside my head so much it was strange for someone to say it out loud.

"I don't know," I said. "I didn't find anything in my room when I came back, and the doctors don't believe me."

Tony looked down and scanned the floor, like the implant would be there, waiting for him to pick it up.

He rolled the chair closer to the bedside. "Here," he said, and thrust out his arm and handed me a manila file folder. A crude drawing of a gray alien head was on the cover, along with the words TOP SECRET. PROJECT ALIEN.

I wanted to laugh but it would've hurt too much. Not so top secret, with ALIEN right there on the cover like that.

"ATIC," Tony said. "Remember? That's what the one guy said when they were talking."

I opened the folder.

"I printed it all out," Tony continued. "From the Internet."

ATIC

Air Technical Intelligence Center

I read down the page:

> The Air Technical Intelligence Center (ATIC), previously known as the Technical Intelligence Division, was a department in the US Air Force responsible for Project Blue Book. After several years it was rebranded as the Aerospace Technical Intelligence Center.

"Project Blue Book," I said. "That's from the 1950s, when they were keeping records of all UFO sightings."

"Yeah, but they're back," Tony said. "They put the project back in commission because people are seeing UFOs again."

I flipped through the pages. "It says here that 'swamp gas' and 'weather conditions' is what the Air Force used to say when people saw UFOs."

"It was a way for them to try to explain it away," Tony said.

"Exactly," I replied. "Make people think they really didn't see anything."

There was a moment of silence.

"So why were those guys out there?" Tony asked. "They were looking for evidence, right? With those radiation detectors?"

"I don't see what else it could mean."

Tony ran a hand through his hair. "This is real, hombre. This is serious."

I set the folder on the nightstand and then took a sip of water. I was tired all of a sudden. I didn't know if it was the painkillers or Dr. Cross's meds.

Tony let out a big breath.

"What do we do now?" he asked.

And I had to admit, that was a good question.

One I didn't have an answer to.

CHAPTER TWENTY-FIVE

OUT OF ALL the books and research I'd read about UFOs and aliens, no one could tell you what to do if you were abducted. Most people had psychological problems and depression. Some of them even tried to commit suicide.

That was not me.

I did not do that.

Two days after Tony came by, I dove back into my Max Holly-oak story. I didn't know what else to do. I didn't feel like playing *EverCraft,* and I didn't want to think about aliens, either. I just wanted to escape. Being back on the pills made me feel disconnected. Out of touch. But I tried to focus as much as I could and write some more words. I just tried to block out everything else that was happening. It was hard, but I did it.

So here's the next part.

Max's dog, Alix, had just told him that his English teacher, Mrs. Evans, could help him.

IV

The Three

Max, Julia, and Sebastian stared at each other across the lunchroom table. They had their own little spot in a far corner, away from the bullies who roamed the cafeteria like meat-eating dinosaurs.

The three of them had met in first grade and had been inseparable ever since. Max couldn't say why, but sometimes they'd even finish each other's thoughts, like twins have been said to do.

They had a lot in common besides being in the same seventh-grade class. All three of them hated gym. They all liked to read. And none of them were popular. And, weirdest of all, over the past weekend, they had all gone through very bizarre experiences. Julia had seen something in her backyard that looked like a gargoyle, and a fortuneteller at the city fair had told Sebastian he was in danger. Not only that, she had said that his friends were in danger too, and called out Max and Julia by name.

Sebastian twirled a braid between his fingers. "So, Alix actually talked? Are you sure?"

Max nodded. He just knew it was Alix. Her mouth hadn't moved, but he'd heard her thoughts in his head. He was certain of it. "She said Mrs. Evans could help," he said, embarrassed that he was telling his friends that his dog actually talked to him.

"What about the man at the park?" Julia asked. "You said he looked weird. Like how?"

Max let out a breath. "He was just, I don't know. He didn't look normal. He had on this dusty old suit and his face was . . ." He trailed off.

Julia fidgeted in her seat. "This *is* weird," she said.

"No kidding," said Sebastian. "That crazy old lady at the fair said we were in danger. She knew your names, too. How could she know that?"

There was a pause. The noise in the lunchroom was roaring, but Max couldn't hear a thing, only the sound of his friends' voices. He looked at Julia. "What do you think it was? That thing you saw outside your window?"

"I don't know," said Julia. "It croaked at me . . . or something."

"What about your parents?" asked Sebastian. "Did you tell them?"

Julia shook her head. "They ran into my room when I screamed, but they said it was probably just a bad dream."

She paused and peered around the cafeteria. "It wasn't," she whispered.

Max slowly tapped one finger on the edge of the table. He glanced at Julia, and then Sebastian. They stared right back at him with blank faces. *How could this be happening? What did it all mean?* "Maybe we should tell Mrs. Evans," he said. "That's, um, what Alix said."

"Well, look who it is. The Dork Patrol."

Max looked up. It was his worst enemy: Molly Crump. Freckles peppered her face, and two red pigtails fell to her shoulders. She wore black cargo pants with a thousand zippers, like she was on some kind of secret mission. Her shirt read **I'M WITH DOOFUS** with an arrow pointing at whoever was unlucky enough to be standing beside her. She quickly reached out and grabbed Julia's carton of milk.

"Hey!" cried Max.

"Oh, I'm all out of milk," said Molly. "You wouldn't want me to go thirsty, would you?" Her eyebrows stitched together as she spoke. Actually, it was one eyebrow, a dirty smudge that crawled across her brow like a fat worm.

"Put it back," said Max firmly.

"It's all right," said Julia. "She probably needs it. I heard milk helps brain cells grow."

Sebastian let out a snort.

"What did you say, Miss Priss?" Molly taunted, drawing closer, towering over Julia like a grizzly bear. She flicked the top of Julia's head with a large finger. *Thwack!*

Max watched as a wave of crimson spread up Julia's neck. "I said . . . put. It. Back!" he growled, his whole body tingling. "Now!"

Bang!

The carton of milk exploded in Molly's hand. Bits of soggy green and white cardboard fluttered down to her big boots. Wet splotches ran down her shirt. Sebastian and Julia stared at Max, their mouths hanging open.

Molly's face turned red as a ripe plum. "Why, you little —" she sputtered. But in the next instant, Mr. Bellasario, Max's history teacher, appeared out of nowhere. He was a huge, hairy man with a bushy, black mustache.

"Miss Crump," he began, "I believe you are all wet." He surveyed the remains of the milk carton on the floor. "Do you not know your own strength?"

Molly just stood there, her mouth open in shock.

"I suggest you get to the ladies' room straightaway," Mr. Bellasario finished.

Molly pointed an accusing finger at Max, her face growing redder by the second. "He did it! It was his fault!"

"*Now*, Miss Crump."

Molly stalked off, pigtails flopping, head sunk low as other kids pointed and giggled.

"As for you three," said Mr. Bellasario, looking at Max over the top of his horn-rimmed glasses, "I advise you to finish your lunch right away. If I hear of another stunt like this, you'll all be in detention." He turned and disappeared into the throng of kids who were chattering about Molly, but not before turning back once to stare at Max, his face taking on an inquisitive look.

Sebastian and Julia turned to Max.

"What did you just do?" Julia whispered. "What was that?"

Max stared at his lunch tray. "I don't know," he said. "It just kind of . . . happened."

Sebastian slid down in his seat. "Now I think we *better* talk to Mrs. Evans," he said.

"Yeah," muttered Max. "I guess so."

I just realized that my character Max Hollyoak is a lot like me. We're both going through something a lot of people would find hard to believe. I think this is what my English teacher meant when she talked about stories being autobiographical. Even if we don't mean to, when we write, our

own experiences just kind of bubble up from our mind somewhere.

I made a promise to myself. Aliens or not, I was going to
finish this book.

No. Matter. What.

CHAPTER TWENTY-SIX

I **FINALLY GOT** the chance to see Miranda when she came over to hang out with Edwin.

"Are you okay?" she asked.

"I guess so," I said.

We were in my room. Miranda sat at my desk while I took a seat on the edge of the bed. She exhaled a long sigh. "Simon. You didn't really try to —"

"Of course I didn't," I cut her off. "I'd never do that. After we came back from our mission, I remembered that I'd been abducted again. The campground wasn't the only time. I had to get it out of me. The implant. I freaked out."

I swallowed, feeling relieved to be telling someone besides Tony what had happened to me.

Miranda scooted over in the rolling desk chair. "What do you remember?" she asked.

I turned away. I really didn't want to talk about it. She seemed to get the hint.

"My dad said there was an article online when you were in the hospital," Miranda said. "Did you hear about it?"

"No," I answered. "What article?"

She dug into her jeans pocket for her phone, then tapped the screen with her thumbs. After a moment, she handed it to me. "Look."

I took the phone and stared.

Glowing Auras and "Black Money"
The Pentagon's Mysterious U.F.O. Program

My heart thudded in my chest.

"It's real," Miranda said. "Official government people are actually talking about it."

I clicked the video that was embedded in the article. It showed a flying white object making impossible maneuvers while being tracked by a Navy F/A-18 Super Hornet. The two pilots could be heard on the video:

> "This is a drone, bro."
> "There's a whole fleet of them. Look on the
> ASA."
> "My gosh!"

"They're all going against the wind. The wind
            is a hundred twenty knots to the west . . ."
"Look at that thing. It's rotating!"

I almost dropped the phone.
This was proof! They were admitting it.
I quickly scanned down the page.

Defense Department . . . $22 million . . .

Advanced Aerospace Threat Identification Program . . .

Started as part of the Defense Intelligence
Agency . . . classified programs . . .

I really couldn't believe it. This was as close to full disclosure as the world was going to get.

"What's your dad say about all this?" I asked.

Miranda looked toward the window. I'd never realized
how long her neck was.

"He says that the time is getting close."

"For what?"

She turned back to me, and her face took on an odd expression, like half joking and half serious. "Oh, you know. I'm sure
he told you all about the alien planet that's going to pass by
Earth and cause destruction."

Nibiru.

She said it like she didn't believe it.

"Yeah," I said. "He did."

Edwin poked his head in the door. "Ready, babe?" he asked.

I jumped.

Miranda shoved her phone back into her pocket and stood up. "See you, Simon. Be careful. Okay?"

"I will," I said, but I wasn't sure what I was supposed to watch out for.

CHAPTER TWENTY-SEVEN

"SIMON."

"*Simon.*"

I looked up. I was studying the little patterns in my blue jeans.

"I asked how you're feeling."

I shrugged. "Okay."

"Just okay?" Dr. Cross repeated, tilting her head. I hated the way she did that. She put on this act that she cared, and I knew she didn't. She was just like all the other adults I knew.

I picked at a loose piece of thread on my jeans. Dr. Cross sat in her chair and looked at me more than she talked. I hated that. She wasn't going to suddenly start believing me, so what was the point? Plus, her office was freezing cold and reminded me of the alien ship with its white walls.

Whir . . . whir . . . click . . . click . . .

"Are you still having uncontrolled thoughts?"

Please leave me alone, I said inside my head.

"How are you sleeping?"

My thoughts were somewhere else. *How could I have gone so long not knowing I was abducted? The government knows. Advanced Aerospace Threat Identification Program. Look at that thing. It's rotating!*

What did they do to me? They wiped my mind or something. Now I remember all of it — the way they walked, the way they studied me, the way they didn't seem to care that I was terrified.

"Simon, talking will help. It's in your own best interest to heal emotionally."

It went on like this for what felt like forever, until finally, my time was up.

My mom thought that seeing Dr. Cross was helping. I know she told Mom that I wasn't talking to her, but Mom never said anything about it. I guess she thought that just going to the psychiatrist's office was better than sitting in my room.

I leaned back against the headboard. The smell of meatloaf drifted up the stairs. I wanted to eat, but I didn't have an appetite. It couldn't go on like this forever, though.

Another thing I didn't want to think about was that school would be starting soon. *How was that even possible?*

AROOO!

I sat up.

AROOO!

"Simon!" Mom called up the stairs. "It's an air drill."

I let out a relieved breath. This wasn't the first time we'd had one. They happen a lot on Air Force bases. It's kind of like a leftover safety precaution from the 1950s. Back then, people thought the atomic bomb could go off at any minute. We learned about it in school. "Duck and Cover," they called it. It was a drill where students had to hide under their desks. I don't know what good that would've done. If an atomic bomb had gone off, everyone would have been freakin' vaporized in an instant, just like Hiroshima and Nagasaki. That was a terrible thing. How could our government have done that to all those people?

I went downstairs, and Mom and I walked out to the front yard. A bunch of our neighbors gathered on their green lawns and mingled together. It was a nice day out. I suddenly thought that maybe I could ride my bike somewhere. But Mom probably wouldn't let me.

I glanced across the street. One of our neighbors, Mr. Diventi, raised a flask to his lips, its silver surface glinting in the sun. I don't like him. Dad says he's an alcoholic. One time, I cut across his lawn to get to school and he came out of his house in his bathrobe and started yelling at me. I told Mom, and when Dad got home from work, he stormed over to Mr.

Diventi's house. When he came back, his face was red. Mom asked him what happened, and Dad said that they'd "had words."

Mr. Diventi never yelled at me again after that.

The sun on the back of my neck felt good. I realized I'd been cooped up for what felt like weeks.

BOOM!

I almost jumped out of my pants.

The ground trembled under my feet, and the windows of all the houses rattled. Mom threw her arms around me in a gesture of protection.

I knew what it was — a sonic boom.

It happened when a plane traveled faster than the speed of sound and created shock waves.

A deafening roar rang in my ears. My head snapped up. Four F-15 planes soared overhead, engines burning a fiery red. It reminded me of the cigarette lighter in Mom's old car that I used to push in and out until she threw it away. The vibrations thundered in my chest. My ears were ringing, and felt like they were about to start bleeding from the pressure in the air. Mom let out a breath and released me. Everybody out on their lawns was gazing up at the sky, shielding their eyes from the sun. We all watched as the jets sped out of sight. Wispy contrails from the burning engines floated above us, like smoke from a fireworks show. I felt weak all of a sudden, like my legs were going to crumple under me.

Air drills and sonic booms were one thing. Screaming F-15 jets overhead were another. That *never* happened.

I asked Dad about it when he got home. "What were they doing? Why was there a sonic boom and then scrambling jets?"

Dad set down his paper and looked at me. "Routine operations, Simon. That's all. Nothing for you to worry about."

I clenched my fist. "What about that article in the *New York Times*? The one about the secret UFO program? Did you see it?"

The sound of Mom chopping vegetables stopped abruptly.

"Ha!" Dad burst out. "Yeah, that's definitely the work of a few sad sacks. Disgruntled employees is what I'd call 'em."

"But there's a video," I persisted. "They said there was a whole fleet of —"

"Simon," Mom turned around. "Stay calm, honey. Don't get upset. I know you and Dr. Cross are talking about this . . . alien stuff. You just have to give it time. Nothing's going to happen to you. Okay?"

She was wrong.

Something was happening.

Something bad.

CHAPTER TWENTY-EiGHT

I **SAT** at the kitchen table, stirring the cereal in my milk. Mom was in the living room, flipping through TV channels with the remote. She seemed different lately — quieter. Maybe she was on meds too, like me. She floated around the house like a ghost or something. I knew it was my fault she was all weirded-out.

I set down the spoon and picked up the *Eagle*, the official paper of the Air Force base. Dad read it every morning. I flipped through it absently, not even really reading anything. I turned to the back page.

AIR BASE YOUTH ARRESTED FOR TRESPASSING

Military Police responded to a call Friday morning from the main gate at 0800 hours, where eighteen-year-old Burke Motley attempted to crash through the barrier in his vehicle. He was apprehended by MPs guarding the entrance. No one was physically harmed in the incident.

"He was extremely agitated," one of the MPs reported. "Talking nonsense. Several times he mentioned 'aliens.'"

Mr. Motley is a Caesar Rodney High School dropout who has had several run-ins with the police and mental health issues over the years, according to his father, Chief Master Sergeant Fred Motley. "I don't know what happened to him," said the senior Motley. "But once he dropped out of school, he started talking about crazy stuff—like UFOs and reptiles living under the earth. He's not a bad kid. I think what he needs is good psychiatric care."

Charges are still pending in the case.

My eyes shifted to the photo that went with the article.

A lean, haunted face stared back at me.

It was Nervy Guy, the dude I met in Miranda's basement.

Burke Motley.

They thought he was crazy.

Was I crazy too?

CHAPTER TWENTY-NINE

EARLY THE NEXT week, I sensed it.

I could almost smell it — hanging in the air like something about to burst.

School was starting in two days.

Two days.

The summer break was almost over, and all I had to show for it was a bunch of pills and an alien abduction.

I didn't want to go back. The thought of gym class was revolting. I didn't want to climb the rope or take a shower with a bunch of bullies. Mom bought me some new pencils, pens, and notebooks. She thought it would cheer me up, like it did when I was little.

It didn't.

Those days were gone.

I decided to write one more chapter of my Max Hollyoak story because once school started, I probably wouldn't have time to work on it. They give us so much homework it's like child abuse.

So here it is. I hope you like it.

The Old Blood

By the end of the day, Max was still flabbergasted by what he had done to Molly in the cafeteria. He sat through the rest of his classes in a daze, staring out of the window. *How could I make a carton of milk explode? How could I hear my dog talking? What's wrong with me?*

When the last bell finally rang, he met Julia and Sebastian at Mrs. Evans's door. She taught English and was his favorite teacher. Most of his classmates thought she was just plain weird. She wore old-fashioned clothes and had a strange way of speaking, like she'd just stepped out of an old history book. She also had the odd habit of disappearing every few days to be replaced by substitute teachers. Max was surprised she hadn't been fired yet.

At least once a week, as all the other kids charged out of school and headed for buses lined up like bright, yellow Legos, Max, Julia, and Sebastian met Mrs. Evans in her classroom, where she read from *The Iliad* and *The Odyssey,* old stories she said were too advanced for the rest of the class. She even sang some parts, her voice soft and high, slender arms raised in the air.

Max loved these after-school lessons, and sometimes it seemed like the stories came to life right there in the classroom: Odysseus and his battle with the Cyclops, a terrifying one-eyed monster; the Sirens — hypnotic creatures who tried to enchant sailors with their eerie songs, hoping to lure them to land; Jason the Argonaut and the Golden Fleece. Now Max was standing at her door, about to tell her a story just as weird.

"Oh, hello children," Mrs. Evans said, rising from her desk as Max and his friends walked into the classroom. "Do we have a reading today? I must've forgotten."

"Um . . . no," Max countered. "We wanted to talk to you about something."

"It's important," added Julia.

A shadow passed over Mrs. Evans's face but quickly faded. "Well, why don't you all have a seat?"

Max, Julia, and Sebastian found seats and dropped their heavy book bags to the floor. Mrs. Evans sat down at one of the student desks and folded her hands in her lap. "Well," she said, "what can I do to help the Amazing Trio?"

No one spoke. Sunlight streamed through the windows, and little dust motes swirled in the air. A silver pendant in the shape of an icicle hung from Mrs. Evans's neck. She usually wore her hair in a fancy knot, but today, Max noticed, it was unbound and fell to her shoulders in waves of black curls. She was also wearing one of her peculiar outfits: a man's tweed suit topped off by a yellow square of silk fabric that bloomed like feathers from her jacket pocket.

Max glanced at Julia and then Sebastian. He coughed. "There was a man who came after me in the park," he began. "I, um, got away from him, but it was really weird."

"And his dog talked to him," added Sebastian.

Max closed his eyes in embarrassment.

Mrs. Evans looked at Max, her green eyes glittering. "And you are sure of this?"

"I'm sure," said Max. "I heard her voice in my head. She said to run, and we ran to a construction site where we hid. And then" — his eyes swept the floor — "she said . . . she said that you could help."

He couldn't believe what he was saying. He knew it had happened, though. It was real.

He watched Mrs. Evans's expression carefully, looking for clues as to whether she thought he was crazy. Her eyes flashed for just a second, but then she nodded calmly, as if regaining her composure. *So Alix was right,* he thought, *she does know something about all this.*

"And where was this place?" Mrs. Evans asked.

"In the woods, by the Botanical Gardens."

"And this . . . man. What did he look like?"

The man's awful mouth sprung up behind Max's eyelids — a slash of red in a pasty face. "He looked out of place — his clothes and stuff. Like out of olden times."

"And he floated after Max," said Julia. "That's what you said earlier, right? And no one else could see him."

Max nodded and clenched his jaw.

Mrs. Evans let out a long breath and looked toward the window. "Was there any . . . iron there, Max? In the park perhaps, or at the construction site?"

Max wrinkled his brow. *Iron? What did iron have to do with anything?* "I think so," he mumbled. "There were a bunch of iron beams lying around."

There was a pause.

"Tell me everything," Mrs. Evans said. "From the beginning."

Over the next twenty minutes, Max and his friends told Mrs. Evans everything that had happened, ending with the exploding milk carton. She took it all in, her large eyes landing on each one of them as they spoke. When they were done, Mrs. Evans glanced toward the window and was silent for what seemed like minutes. Max, Julia, and Sebastian traded glances.

"I thought it would have lasted much longer," Mrs. Evans said quietly.

"Huh?" said Max.

"What would have lasted longer?" said Julia and Sebastian at the same time.

Mrs. Evans didn't answer, but rose from her seat and closed the door. She drew the blinds, and darkness immediately fell on the room. Max exchanged a glance with Julia and Sebastian.

Mrs. Evans walked back over to the small chair and sat down. "I've always said that the three of you are special," she began, "and what I am about to say now will seem very hard to believe."

Max leaned forward in his seat.

"Did you ever wonder why you are all so close to each other?" she started. "Why you are the only children in your families? Why you sometimes complete each other's sentences?" She turned to Julia and Sebastian.

I never told her about that, thought Max. *The way we all kind of know what each other's thinking.*

They all shrugged, and a murmur of *I-don't-know*s and *it-just-happen*s came from their mouths.

"You are connected by a bond stronger than you could imagine," she said.

Mrs. Evans stood up, walked to her desk, and bent down

to open the bottom cabinet. She withdrew a tattered brown leather book. Max caught a glimpse of strange black marks on the cover. She flipped through the pages and, after a moment, began to read, her voice soft, yet full of power:

> *"Born of two worlds, but belonging to none*
> *The old blood stirs within.*
> *Staff, Chain, and Sword they will bear*
> *The old blood stirs within.*
> *Evil shall fall, when three are called.*
> *When the old blood stirs within."*

She closed the book. Max watched a small cloud of dust escape from its crumbly pages.

"And that would mean . . . what?" asked Sebastian.

Mrs. Evans's gaze rested on Sebastian. "Have you ever heard of faeries?" she asked with a straight face.

Sebastian burst into a wide grin. "Faeries? Like Tinker Bell? Yeah, sure."

"Children's stories," Julia added.

Max remained silent.

"Long ago," Mrs. Evans continued, sitting down again, "in the early days of the world, there was a race of people called the Twilight Folk. They took humans into the faerie realm and kept them there until they forgot the mortal world and sometimes even their own names."

Max's ears perked up.

"But over time, humans became more and more evil, and they corrupted the fae with their desire for greed, violence, and other things" — she turned away a moment — "too terrible to mention."

Max nodded blankly, but had no idea what Mrs. Evans was talking about.

"Fae?" he asked.

"It is just another way of saying faerie, Max. Fae, fee, fair folk. It is all the same."

"Oh," he said, wondering where this was all leading.

"Now, after many years, the fae shunned the mortal race, and humans were banished from the realm, never to return. And as the years passed, humankind forgot them and they became but a memory, something from the daydreams of the very young."

Max blinked. Something was stirring inside of him. A warm glow he couldn't describe.

"But," Mrs. Evans continued, holding up a slim finger, "before the banishment, when the two races still met, they would sometimes fall in love, and the children they bore were beautiful to look upon."

Max swallowed hard. "Children?"

"Yes. The children of faeries and humans."

"Okay, this is weird," said Julia, screwing up her face.

A sad smile played along Mrs. Evans's lips. "Perhaps so, Julia, but the desire for love crosses all boundaries."

Max thought she looked sad all of a sudden. After a moment, she looked back up. "So, the bloodline of the fae passed into the human world, but over the years, it grew weak and died out. But now, something magical has happened. Something —" Her eyes landed on Max. "Extraordinary."

"What?" said Max, almost afraid to hear the answer.

Mrs. Evans paused. "Three children have been found who possess the old blood."

No one spoke.

"Faerie blood," she said.

Max sat stunned.

"Do you understand?" she continued, her eyes lighting up. "You are human children born with faerie blood. You are the three of which the poem speaks."

The clock on the wall *tick-tock*ed as loud as a hammer stroke in Max's ears. He couldn't believe what he had just heard. Mrs. Evans was someone he trusted, and he couldn't imagine why she would play such a strange joke on him.

Sebastian stared at the closed blinds, speechless for once. Julia took a sudden interest in her lap.

Mrs. Evans studied Max's face. "Long have we watched over you, Max. That is why I was sent here. But now, with these . . . encounters, we must act quickly. The enemy is moving."

"What 'enemy'?" said Max.

"What do you mean 'watched'?" asked Julia.

"'Sent here'?" added Sebastian.

Mrs. Evans stood up again and seemed to grow taller, a vast shadow filling the room. She clutched the icicle pendant that hung from her neck. Max watched in fascination as she twirled it between her fingers so quickly it became a blur. A dot of red within the pendant began to glow, and the room grew darker. Max gasped as the ceiling tiles vanished and a black sky appeared overhead, winking with stars, just like in a planetarium.

A forest appeared in the black canvas, gleaming with silver trees. Max looked on in amazement as a swirling flood of images took shape: a red stag with black antlers bent low to drink from a still lake, white mist streaming from its nostrils; women in fancy dresses and long white gloves up to their elbows stepped from horse-drawn carriages; small creatures with wings like stained glass flew above an old gray mansion with candles flickering in the windows. A myriad of colors danced around the room, sparkling shades of green, red, and gold. Creatures Max couldn't describe peeked from the corners of the vision with bright eyes and odd grins.

"Behold!" Mrs. Evans cried.

The three children shrunk back.

Max watched in awe as Mrs. Evans . . . *changed*. Her eyes, already the shape of perfect almonds, grew larger and deeper, like a cat's. Her ears rose into sharp points. As if by magic, she now held upraised in one hand a staff of rough wood etched with symbols: a swan, a hawk, and what looked to Max like a tree in bloom. "My name is Elspeth," she said, raising her arms in the dark room. "I am from the Court of the Morning. I am of the fae."

"Aieee!" Sebastian yelped and bolted for the door, sending his desk clattering across the room. Mrs. Evans made an intricate motion with her left hand and the lock snapped shut with a click. Sebastian rattled the doorknob back and forth, but it wouldn't open.

"There is no denying it, Sebastian," Mrs. Evans said. "You are a Twilight Child. Your life is forever changed. Korrigan, the King of the Night Court, is searching for you. I am your only hope."

Julia gasped and jumped from her seat to follow

Sebastian, but Max reached out and grabbed her wrist. Julia paused, but was still poised to run.

Max glanced warily at Mrs. Evans. Her face was severe, but the compassion he knew so well was still reflected in her eyes. *I have to trust her,* he thought. *I have to.*

"Sebastian," he said quietly, "come back."

Sebastian slowly released his hand from the doorknob, then walked back over and sat down. Julia let out a long sigh and stared at Mrs. Evans in amazement.

As for Max, he finally had an answer to a question he had never asked.

Now he knew why he was different.

CHAPTER THIRTY

MY FIRST DAY back at school was terrible. I walked down the
hallway and took in all the familiar faces — the bullies, the
sports stars, the quiet kids like me. The drab beige walls and
gray lockers just made me feel depressed. Plus, it *smelled* like
school. I passed an open janitor's closet and the eye-burning
scent of cleaning supplies almost made me pass out. It mingled
with the aroma of food in the cafeteria, and I felt like I was
going to barf. Do I even need to mention the bathrooms?

Somehow, I made it through the first part of the day without losing my mind and met up with Tony during lunch.

"Hey, hombre," he said, and waved me over to sit next to
him in the cafeteria. The sound of a thousand kids screaming
and hollering was unbearable. Mom had packed me a bologna
and cheese sandwich. It was all smooshed up in the Ziploc bag.

"You gonna eat that?" Tony asked.

I pushed it over to him. "Sweet," he said.

Tony took the sandwich out of the bag and took a huge bite. "Any news?" he asked, his mouth full.

"Like what?"

"I don't know." Tony looked left, then right, then lowered his voice. "Have you seen anything else? Any aliens or anything?"

"No."

There was a moment of silence. "I was thinking," he said. "Your dad works around jets and stuff, right? In the Ninth Airlift Squadron? He might know something about this UFO program."

I shook my head. "Are you serious? He'd never tell me anything. He doesn't believe in UFOs, anyway."

"Hmpf," Tony muttered, still chewing. "What about those F-15s? The sonic booms and all that?"

"My dad said it was routine operations," I said.

"So did mine," Tony answered. "Do you believe him?"

"No. I don't."

"Neither do I."

CHAPTER THIRTY-ONE

I **SAT** in Dr. Cross's office, freezing my butt off. My appointments with her were always the same, like a bad dream, or that movie *Groundhog Day*, where the guy wakes up and has to live through the same thing over and over again.

Here's how it went: me sitting in a too-big chair and Dr. Cross studying my every move.

"So," Dr. Cross started. "I've been doing some reading."

Congratulations, I wanted to say.

She shifted in her seat. "Some psychologists believe that alien abductions are really people having what are called hypnagogic hallucinations."

I'd never heard those words before.

"Their studies show that when people are in this . . . hypnagogic state, they can see, hear, and smell things as if they're awake, when they're not."

Dr. Cross rested a finger on her cheek. "Now, Simon, when this . . . abduction occurred, you said that you couldn't move. Is that correct?"

I didn't want to answer, but I did. "Yes," I croaked out.

She gave a half smile — relieved, I guess, that I'd finally opened up a little. She leaned forward. "Simon, this could be sleep paralysis. A feeling of being consciously awake but unable to move." She paused. "That would also explain the bed-wetting."

I cringed, embarrassed.

She steepled her fingers and leaned back. "The sooner we understand what's happening, the better you'll feel. None of this is your fault, Simon. The mind is a strange and beautiful thing. Sometimes it plays tricks on us, and we have to treat that as an illness. Do you understand?"

I picked at a worn spot on my jeans and nodded my head just a bit.

Dr. Cross smiled. It wasn't just a regular smile. She was practically beaming. I knew she'd tell Mom that we'd had a breakthrough. She'd hold a freakin' news conference announcing Alien Boy had finally broken his silence.

But she didn't get it.

I wasn't under some kind of hypna — whatever she called it.

It was real.

I knew it.

And I had the scar to prove it.

CHAPTER THIRTY-TWO

I **SAT** in science class trying to keep my eyes open. My head kept falling to my chest every few seconds. I was wiped out. Being back on the pills made me tired.

A long time ago, Dr. Cross said it would take a while for the pills to stabilize. Maybe that didn't happen before because I stopped taking them. Now I had to go through the whole thing all over again.

I really hated the feeling.

I still wasn't sleeping well. Maybe the aliens had come for me again and I didn't even know it. It took me weeks to realize I'd been abducted before. Maybe it had happened again.

Mr. Sofio's droning voice was doing nothing to keep me awake. He was talking about something called a sling psychrometer. I had no idea what it was. *Some kind of tool to measure humidity?*

"Okay," he suddenly announced. "Field trip. Everyone

grab their belongings and follow me out to the green-house."

I flinched at the loud scrapes and commotion as everyone got up and grabbed their stuff. I usually liked trips to the greenhouse, which were a regular part of the class, but that day, I just wanted to put my head down on the desk and sleep.

Outside, it was hot, and I immediately felt my chest tighten. Mr. Sofio took long strides through the grass, like some kind of giant stork. "High humidity today," he announced, to no one in particular.

The greenhouse was behind the football field, surrounded by a small patch of woods. Sunlight glinted off the glass panes of the roof as we approached. Inside, the ceiling was curved, like the skeleton of a ribbed animal. I imagined for a second that it was a dragon. The humidity clung to my skin like a fine mist. My glasses fogged up immediately, and when I wiped them on my shirt, it made them even grimier than they were before.

Rows and rows of containers and pots lined the tables. Small lights on wires shone down from above. Little trays of pebbles sat under a lot of the plants, and others were protected from sunlight by shade cloths.

Mr. Sofio rummaged around in his bag and took out some supplies, including the sling psychrometer. It smelled damp in there. Damp and musty. Kids were joking and talking loudly. Some of the quieter ones, like me, just stood around, wondering what to do with our hands. There were a few hard, wooden benches, and I was about to sit down, but then —

A flapping sound.

Rustling.

Wings.

My heart jumped in my chest.

Heads turned upward, searching.

"What was that?" Jason Milford asked.

Mr. Sofio scanned the corners of the ceiling.

"There's the culprit," he said.

I looked up.

Something gray. Black eyes.

My face got hot. My hands trembled. I swallowed and reached for my inhaler. I couldn't breathe.

"Somebody get it!" Mindy Clayton burst out.

"It's not hurting anybody!" shouted Cathy Taylor, the girl Tony used to tease me about.

The bird swooped down in a flurry of gray feathers. It was coming for me.

"No!" I screamed. "Keep it away!"

I fell back into the table. Containers and pots clattered to the floor. In my effort to get up, I slipped in a puddle of water and went down again.

"Simon," Mr. Sofio said, leaning over me. "Are you all right?"

He offered a hand and pulled me up. The back of my pants was wet.

A bunch of students were gathered by the door. Whatever it was must have flown out. Their voices filled the room:

"Just some dumb bird."

"Some kind of hawk or something."

"It wasn't a hawk, it was an owl."

"In the daytime? Owls are nocturnal, doofus."

And then the stares and giggles began.

"Simon's a douche. Did you see him?"

"Somebody peed his pants."

"Aieee!" Billy Hampton cried out, mocking me.

"That's enough," Mr. Sofio scolded him.

My glasses had steamed up again. I was standing there like a dork, frozen, while they hurled insults.

Mr. Sofio held me by the elbow. "Okay, Simon? Did you have an asthma attack? Do you want to see the nurse?"

"*Nurse*," Billy snickered.

"No," I choked out. "I'm okay."

I stood there, my face damp, my breath coming in short gasps. I took my inhaler from my pocket and gave myself a dose. *One . . . two . . . three . . . exhale.*

I felt all of their eyes on me.

I was a freak.

A loser.

Worst of all, Cathy Taylor just stared at me like I was some kind of idiot.

CHAPTER THIRTY-THREE

I **LEFT SCHOOL** early. I didn't even tell anyone, and when I got home, Mom didn't seem to notice. She was in her bedroom watching TV. She was doing that more and more lately, like she was sinking into her own little private world. It was all my fault.

The insults from the greenhouse came back to me, echoing in my ears: *Simon's a douche. Somebody peed his pants.*

And then Mr. Sofio: *Do you want to see the nurse?*

God, it was embarrassing.

I'd never be able to live it down. The only thing worse would've been if I'd *really* peed my pants.

Dad was at work, as usual, and wasn't coming home for dinner. He calls it "having chow in the mess hall." Before I actually saw a mess hall, I imagined it as some kind of giant room with a bunch of military guys having a food fight, like in that movie *Animal House*, another one I wasn't supposed to watch but did anyway with Tony one time when his parents were away.

Dad only took me to his work once, when I was little, after I'd bugged him about it for weeks. This was when we lived on a different Air Force base. Ohio, I think. I'd gone through this phase where I was obsessed with airplanes, and Mom finally convinced him to take me. We had to get a special pass because not even family members were allowed on that section of the base. There were guys standing around with guns and helmets and handcuffs and other police gear. They looked pretty tough, and I was afraid to look them in the eyes.

Dad brought me to this huge hangar where giant cargo planes sat like sleeping dinosaurs. We got close to one called a C-5, and it was so big I didn't want to get any closer. I couldn't imagine how something that big and heavy could lift up and fly for thousands of miles. It was Dad's job to stack boxes on wooden pallets and then lift them up with a forklift into the plane. When I asked him what was in the boxes, he said he couldn't tell me. He said it was a matter of national security. I wasn't sure if he was kidding or not.

The guys inside the hangar reminded me of a bunch of worker bees because they all moved around so quickly. "Everyone has a part to play," I remember Dad saying, his hands on his hips. "That's the key to any organization, Simon. It has to run like a well-oiled machine."

After he showed me around the cargo bays, he brought me to the mess hall, where we ate lunch. I had a burger and fries. All of his friends came by and rubbed my head or slapped me on the shoulders. They all talked just like Dad and had names like Rusty, Cole, and Hank. "Hey, kiddo," they'd said, or, "What's up, champ?"

It was cheesy, but I didn't mind. I've always remembered that day because it's one of the few really good times I've had with Dad. After that, when I grew up and wasn't into sports or anything, we didn't really connect.

The door creaked open, and Mom came in carrying a tray of food. "How's a grilled cheese sandwich sound?"

"Not really hungry," I answered, but as she set the tray down, I saw it also held a bowl full of potato chips and a glass of Coke. She never bought that kind of stuff at the commissary. Dad said it was all sugar and salt and who knew what else. He was right, I guess.

"It'll be our little secret," Mom assured me.

I wolfed down the grilled cheese sandwich. I hadn't realized how hungry I was until I started eating. I guzzled the Coke and stuffed my face with the chips. Mom looked at me like I was nuts. "Slow down there, cowboy," she said, another one of her corny lines. I have to admit, though, I kind of like her dumb Mom sayings.

After I finished, she left and came back in with the pill bottles. She watched me swallow each one, and her face looked sad. It was my fault she had to do this. I wanted to tell her that she didn't have to watch me — that I wasn't going to let her down again, that I would take the pills — but I didn't.

I'm not really sure she would've believed me, to tell the truth.

That night, I plugged in the unicorn night-light and tried to go to sleep. I stared at it, glowing yellowish-green in the pitch-black. I turned over on my side. I kept hearing the snickering voices from the greenhouse, chattering. Mocking me.

Simon's a douche. Did you see him?

Somebody peed his pants.

Hoo hoo.

I bolted up.

What was that?

I whipped my head toward the window.

It was an owl. Sitting on the ledge. But it was outside.

Hoo hoo.

Another owl swooped down and joined it.

They were staring at me, swiveling their heads in that weird way they do.

Hoo hoo.

A flash of light filled the room.

I threw my hands up in front of my face, shielding my eyes. I peeked between my fingers.

One of the owls was suddenly sitting at the foot of my bed. It was *inside* the house.

Watching me.

Waiting.

I tried to move.

I was frozen.

They were back!

Help! I shouted, but just like before, my mouth didn't move. I felt the same familiar tingling. All over my body. I didn't know if I was sitting up or lying back.

The owl hopped up the sheet toward me.

I tried to pull the covers over my face.

HOO HOO.

The light in the room was flickering, even though there was only a night-light. A crackly, electric zapping was in my ears.

The owl seemed to be growing.

HOO HOO.

OH MY GOD.

It stretched itself. It was turning into something.

It wasn't an owl.

Spindly arms and legs . . . an almond-shaped head . . .

It was a Gray.

I felt a vibration all through my body. A long finger reached out and touched the center of my forehead.

Zap!

White-hot light filled the room.

Please God help me

Please God help me

Please God help me

Please God help—

I was back on the ship again.

Whir . . .

Click . . .

A tall gray alien was standing over me.

The General, I remembered calling him. He was the leader.

SILENCE. REMAIN IN POSITION.

What did that mean!

Whir . . .

Click . . .

I felt like a rabbit in a cage—nervous and wild-eyed. But not able to move. *No one should have to go through this. No one!*

The General leaned toward me. I felt the darkness of those eyes searing into my soul—two black orbs that led to who knew where.

REMAIN CALM, I heard.

And then he poked me in the stomach where the implant had been.

CHAPTER THIRTY-FOUR

I *DIDN'T KNOW* where I was.

Dim yellow light filled the space I was in.

There.

A window—a long, curved piece of what looked like glass, fading out of vision.

I was lying down.

The General's face appeared above me again, floating, like some sort of projection.

Was he really there, or was it a picture?

Behind him, a curtain of fathomless black unspooled like a ribbon, stars and planets winking within its depths.

WE SERVE THE GALAXIES FROM BEYOND, I heard inside my head.

His thin lips didn't move, but I sensed his voice loud and clear. It was flat. Emotionless.

Alien.

I can try to talk to him. If I can hear him, maybe he can hear me.

I formed a sentence in my head:

WHAT DO YOU WANT? WHY ARE YOU DOING THIS?

The black mass of stars and swirling colors behind him flared and then dimmed.

HUMANITY IS BEYOND REPAIR.

The black shadows rippled, like a giant wave.

WE HAVE TRIED TO HELP YOU EVOLVE. BUT WE ARE MET BY IGNORANCE.

I swallowed. My tongue felt as heavy as a brick.

NOT ALL OF US, *I said inside my head.* SOME OF US BELIEVE.

A pause, and then . . .

YOU HAVE BEEN CHOSEN. YOU WILL EVOLVE.

What did that mean? What were they going to do to me?

The face floated closer. The eyes were getting bigger, pushing into my brain. I tried to close my own eyes, but my vision was suddenly filled with a spinning golden disc. It made no sound, but eclipsed everything else in sight.

Markings were etched onto its surface: squiggly lines, squares, circles, and other symbols I didn't recognize.

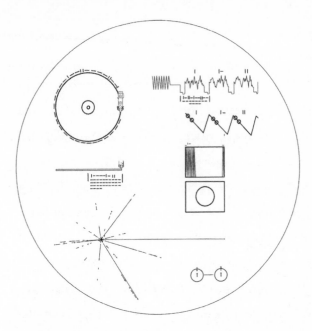

And then I heard sounds.

Sounds that grew louder and louder until they turned into a great chorus, like a choir I heard when Mom took me to church one time. The voices were beautiful, lifting and soaring words that I couldn't recognize, and they seemed to fill my whole body up with white light.

Is this what angels sound like? I wondered.

The chorus faded. There was a moment where I didn't hear anything at all, and then —

I heard laughter from old TV shows. The sad cry of whale songs. Different languages all being spoken at the same time, one on top of the other, growing and building. I thought of the

Tower of Babel story from the Bible and how God separated the languages of mankind.

I heard the barking of dogs and the mewling of cats. The rat-a-tat-tat of Morse code and the screaming of chimpanzees. Trumpeting elephants, braying donkeys, the songs of birds, and the cries of eagles and hawks.

And then it dawned on me. I knew what I was hearing. We'd learned about it in school. It was called the Golden Record and it had been sent into the cosmos with the Voyager spacecraft a long time ago by NASA. It was kind of like sending a message in a bottle across the sea, but instead, this record traveled across the universe. Maybe one day it would be found by another species and they could learn who we were and where we came from.

Had the Grays gotten the message?

Did we lead them here?

Something rang in my head. It was like a bell, but deeper, heavier. I felt it in my whole body.

TRANSMITTING MESSAGE, I heard.

Images flashed in front of my eyes. Numbers and symbols and notes and markings I had never seen before and could make no sense of. With my eyes closed, this is what I saw:

ˈU:ˈU·ˈW::ˈW·ˈb·ˈbↄ⊕ꞆↄꝭↄꝭↄꞆↄↄ:⊃Ꞁⴹ·⊃⊇Ⴑↄↄ:⊃ꞀⴹˈWↃ∪Ↄ⊕ ꝭↄꞆↄ⊄ⴹ
ꝭↄⴹꞆↄⴹↃⴹ:∪:⊃:⊃ⴹⴹ :ꓴⴹⴹꞆↄ ˈⴥˈⴥ∪ˈⴥↃˈ∪ˈⴥˈ|:ꝭↄↄⴥↄↄↄↄ Ꞇↄↄↄↄↄ ∪ⴹ Ꞇↄꝭ∪ⴹↄ
ꝭↄꞀↄ⊄ↄↄ:Ↄↄↄ∪ꝭↄↄⴹ⊕ↄↄↄↄↄↄⴹ‖‖

The pressure in my head felt as cold as ice and as hot as flame at the same time.

It pulsed.

Then the images flashed out. There was a dark, quiet stillness. My ears were ringing. But I knew that something was different now. I sensed it, and then I felt it swarming in my head.

I knew everything.

My head was overflowing with knowledge.

I saw the stars being born and the swirling galaxies of deepest space.

I saw our place in the universe from way, way above — tiny green and blue little Earth, floating in space. So small. So fragile.

I heard the whisper of languages in my ears, all languages, a constant murmuring.

I saw the first sea — a blue ocean teeming with life.

I saw comets and meteors and asteroids and black holes and the rings of Saturn being formed.

I saw the microscopic beginnings of life, squirming and swimming in green algae.

I saw strands of DNA and starlight, flaring bright in the heavens.

I was above it all now — floating, looking into the deepest mysteries of space.

We were part of a giant cosmos. Just one tiny speck. But we were unique. Special. One link in a chain of galaxies and planets that all worked together.

Next I saw humans. Humans in all of their pain and chaos.

War.

Disease.

Global warming.

I knew what it all meant.

Earth was dying.

It was too late now. We'd had our chance.

I wanted to cry.

Wanted to tell everyone that we were destroying the planet.

But it was too late.

We messed up.

But there is a way, *I suddenly realized. First I felt it, and then it was shown to me like a great tree, with branches forking out at many angles, each one holding what I somehow understood to be mankind's potential future path. One of them showed humans as an evolved species, living in peace and exploring distant galaxies.*

The face of the General appeared again. I wanted to ask him about what I had just seen, and why it was being shown to me. I had so many questions! But his face faded, leaving only a faint outline of stars.

• • •

I turned over. Something was wrong. The bed was cold . . . damp.

No!

Wet sheets!

That meant that they'd come again!

I couldn't remember . . . everything was foggy. My mouth tasted like metal.

But then —

HUMANITY IS BEYOND REPAIR.

The words rang in my head like a warning.

"Simon," Mom called from downstairs, "can you get online? My phone's not working."

They'd come again!

I scrambled out of bed and bolted down to the living room, still in my underwear.

"Simon," Mom said. She was standing in the kitchen in her nightgown. "What's going on? Where are your pajamas?"

"They're coming," I said.

"Who?"

"The aliens. The Grays."

AROOOOOO! AROOOOO!

I flinched as a piercing siren rang in my ears.

"It's just another air drill," Mom said. "Calm down, Simon."

"No," I gasped. "It's happening. They came again last night. The General said humanity was beyond repair!"

I heard footsteps on the stairs. My pulse raced. It was Edwin in his robe, running his fingers through his messy hair. "What's going on?" he asked.

Static electricity tingled all over my body, like tiny pins and needles.

"Who?" Mom asked. "Simon, what general? What are you talking about?"

The landline rang. I grabbed it. "Hello?" I said. "*Hello?*"

"Simon." Dad's voice came through the phone, but the line was crackly and filled with static. The lights in the kitchen began to flicker. Mom looked to the ceiling, her eyes a little alarmed.

"Simon," Dad said, "do not leave the house. Put your mother on."

"What's going on?" I asked. "Dad. What's happening?"

"Simon!" he shouted. "Put your mother on *NOW!*"

AROOO! AROOO!

I handed Mom the phone. She took it slowly, like I was handing her a live snake.

"Hello?" she said. "Honey? What's happening?"

Mom stood there a moment, nodding, and then her eyes went wide. She looked up at me. "We have to go to the basement," she said. "Now!"

"Is it another air drill?" Edwin asked, and even his voice seemed a little off, not the usual tough-guy attitude.

I had to know what was happening. I rushed to the door.

Mom reached out to stop me, but I zipped past her.

"Simon!" she called out, running after me. "Don't open the door!"

But I did.

And I looked up.

It was morning, but it was dark. The clouds were purple.

I was right!

Right, all along.

And no one had believed me.

A massive black ship hung in the sky.

Tentacles of light writhed along the bottom of it, like a tangle of snakes, searching, probing.

Mist rose all around it, like it had brought the clouds down from the sky.

And then it made a sound.

A sound like breaking glass and cannon bursts and crashing waves and air drills and sonic booms all mixed together.

WE ARE HERE, I heard inside my head.

WE

HAVE

COME.

ONE HUNDRED YEARS LATER

THE SUN BEAT DOWN on the green grass and warmed Simon's face. His hair was white, but the years had been kind to him. A youthful twinkle could still be found in his eyes.

He looked up, and the puffy white clouds above brought a memory from when he was a child, long ago.

Before they came.

He remembered looking up into a blue sky and letting his imagination run wild. He would find pictures in the clouds —a ship, a knight, a sea cresting with foamy waves. That was so long ago now. He barely remembered.

It was another life. Another time.

The children gathered around him were wide-eyed and inquisitive, always wanting to learn and grow, and, above all, to avoid repeating the errors of their ancestors.

Simon was one of the Appointed, the children around him knew—those fortunate few who were tasked with leading humankind into a new age of peace and prosperity.

There was no more war.

No more pain.

No more disease.

There was only one race.

The human race.

Simon's family was still with him, as well as his friends Tony and Miranda. Edwin and his parents had been resistant at first, especially his father, whose whole world and belief system was shattered when the Grays came. But Simon had led them to a path of understanding.

We had called them the Grays because we didn't have another name for them.

But they were the Annunaki, the Gods of the Sky.

The abductions, the UFO sightings, the encounters with humans over the years — they'd all been attempts to understand us, Simon had learned. The false memories they planted were ways to try to ease our trauma in experiencing something beyond our capacity. The differences in our intelligence were vast. Simon understood it to be similar to trying to explain physics to Cro-Magnon man. That was what it was like for them. They were of a higher form and came to help humanity evolve.

"Tell us the story again," one of the children asked. She was a New Colony child, those born within the first hundred years of the Grays' arrival, and bearing all the signs of the new human species. Her skin was brown, and her eyes, two fathomless pools of black, drew Simon in.

"Yes," piped in another — a boy with long, graceful limbs and the same eyes as the girl who sat next to him. "Tell us about *Max Hollyoak and the Tree of Everwyn.*"

Simon leaned back and swept a hand through his hair. He smiled. He'd told the story many times before, but it had never become a burden, and he doubted it ever would.

"Okay," he said, "just one more time . . .

". . . Max, Julia, and Sebastian made their way through the darkening woods. The sky above them was bruised and swollen, as if filled with the hopes and dreams of those who had fallen.

But still, Max and his companions had won.

They were the Twilight Children.

Korrigan, the King of the Night Court, had fallen.

Elspeth, the Queen of the Court of the Morning, had told Max and his friends they were special. There were many like them, and in every story, if you knew where to look, he or she could be found. A hero, waiting to be born.

'You will change,' she had told them. 'But you will always survive.'

The strong will always survive."

THE END